Susan Hill was b................................ough. Her family
moved to Coventry when she was sixteen and she read for a
degree in English at King's College, London. Her first and
second novels were published when she was an undergraduate
and she is now a Fellow of King's.

She won The Somerset Maugham Award for her novel *I'm
the King of the Castle*, the John Llewellyn Rhys Prize for *The
Albatross* and *The Bird of Night* won the Whitbread Award and
was shortlisted for The Booker Prize.

She has written over thirty books, including the autobio-
graphical books *The Magic Apple Tree*, and *Family*, a number of
children's books, and the celebrated ghost story *The Woman in
Black*. The play adapted from this has been running in
London's West End for eighteen years and plays around the
world.

Most recently Susan Hill has been writing a sequence of
contemporary crime novels set in the English Cathedral town
of Lafferton and featuring DCI Simon Serrailler.

She has written three volumes of short stories, including in
2002, the highly-praised collection *The Boy Who Taught the
Beekeeper to Read*.

Susan is married to the Shakespeare scholar Stanley Wells.
They have two adult daughters and live in a farmhouse in
Gloucestershire.

Susan Hill may be contacted via her website
www.susan-hill.com or via *www.longbarnbooks.com*.

FARTHING HOUSE
and other stories

by

SUSAN HILL

LONG BARN BOOKS

PUBLISHED BY
LONG BARN BOOKS

Ebrington Gloucestershire GL55 6NW

Some of the stories in this collection were
previously published in *A Bit of Singing and Dancing*
and *The Albatross and Other Stories.*

Set in Adobe Garamond
Cover by Design Holborn
Printed and Bound by Compass Press Ltd

ISBN 1 902 421 124

CONTENTS

KIELTY'S   7

MR PROUDHAM AND MR SLEIGHT   31

THE CUSTODIAN   45

HALLORAN'S CHILD   83

HOW SOON CAN I LEAVE?   109

THE BADNESS WITHIN HIM   129

RED AND GREEN BEADS   143

FARTHING HOUSE   153

THE ALBATROSS   173

KIELTY'S

That day, Jed had done what was forbidden. He had been up to Kielty's. But, he thought, it doesn't matter because they won't know and they can't find out. Not now.

It had been almost dark by the time he got home, no one at all had seen him as he ran and tomorrow, he and Ma were leaving very early on the train for Tadley and that was more than eight miles away. There would be no time for questions, and there was never any danger of Da meeting a Kielty and hearing about it that way. Da did not talk to Kieltys.

'They can't find out.' He whispered the words out loud, for reassurance, and the words lay there upon the darkness. He heard them. He thought that in some way he might even see or touch them.

'They can't find out. They won't ever know.'

Besides, it hadn't really been his fault. Not really. He had been going mad with the restlessness of waiting for tomorrow, for the slow, magic journey and the first sight of black chimneys and brickworks, the long, long streets of sooted house and the trams and the coal-pit gantries, the butcher's shop that belonged to his Uncle Wilberforce. In the end, Ma had packed him out from under her feet, sick of his fretting about between room and room and of poking into the luggage and asking the time every five minutes.

'Can't you see how much I've got to do? Leave me be child.'

So it was her fault, wasn't it, that he had gone down the lanes beating at the keck and spear grasses with a stick out of boredom with the country and longing for the town and had gone farther than he would ever dare to go on any normal day; her fault that he had met Finn Kielty, carrying a bale of wire over his shoulder.

'Is it for a hen run?'

'Hens run out in't yard.'

'What's it for then?'

'Fox.'

Finn Kielty had one eye that looked straight at you and one that always looked some other way, it was perhaps because of that, as well as for the sores on his arms, which he was scratching now that he, like all Kieltys, was always kept at a distance.

'What fox?'

'Found it in a gin-trap in Thwaites wood last night. Not hurt bad enough to shoot so Kielty's making a run. He'll keep it while it's set up again.'

Not even his children called him anything but Kielty.

'Foxes are wild. They go for you.'

'Never. Tame as a babby, or will be soon enough. Kielty tames anything. He's a way of talking to them. We'd a badger one time.'

Kielty out with a gun in Thwaites Wood, Jed thought. Poaching.

'Is that how an honest man gets by?' Da had said. 'Thievin' and odd-jobbin'. Is that a decent way to rear a family?'

Because Da worked from morning till night, had done for years, to set himself up and not be beholden.

Finn Kielty picked up the wire and put it on his shoulder again. 'Coming up to see it then?'

Jed stared at him and then away, up the hill towards that forbidden place. 'Nobody goes up Kielty's.'

But he wanted to, and not just to see the lame fox either.

Words ran through his head for the first time, teasing. 'They can't find out. They won't know.'

Finn Kielty was waiting. If it weren't for the eyes looking their different ways and unsettling you he had a nice face, Jed thought, a good, nice face.

'All right then.'

So he went beside Finn, who was three years older but not much taller, along the lane towards the hill, and it was as though his legs were filled only with air, he could not feel the hard ground under him and his heart thumped the blood so hard through his chest and up into his head that he feared it might somehow burst out of him.

At the very top of Hapton Hill was the old windmill with one sail, and beyond that, up a track, was where Kielty's lived. Once, long before Jed had been born, before Da and Ma even came here. It had been a farm and the farmhouse had had a proper name but now everyone said, 'Up there', nodding, or 'Up Kielty's.' Because of what they thought of him and because he only rented the place, with some sheds and a rough couple of acres round it.

No one knew where Kielty had come from. 'Irish.' But he didn't talk like that. Nor did anyone know for truth that the woman who lived with him was not his wife and half the children not his own, though it was what they all said and whenever Jed heard it and asked questions Da and Ma stopped talking about it straight away, or sent him outside.

Some people had grow used to Kielty's. 'Live and let live.' And it was surely only common charity, Ma said, to give them good-day if you met them face to face. But not to go up there. Never.

'And don't you sit next to any of them in school.'

'We sit where we get put.'

'Then lean the other way.'

'Why?'

'Isn't it enough that I've told you to?'

But Tess Pinker said it was because Kielty's had nits in their hair, she'd seen them jump when Dorry Kielty flicked up a plait, and fleas as well, and that the scabs on Finn Kielty's arms were rat bites.

'Nits is catchin' and rat bites is poison. Up Kielty's is like a midden.'

'Have you been?'

'Don't talk daft Jed Blaker. Nobody goes up Kielty's.'

But now he had.

He started awake out of a dream about the place and as he sat up in bed he saw that the moon was full riding above Hapton Hill; it shone onto his face, onto the broken sail of the windmill. Onto Kielty's. 'Stare into the moon long enough and you go mad.' So he lay down again quickly and turned his face towards the door to be safe. Though Ma told him not to believe half of what he heard and especially not what Aunt Hatt in Todley said, you could never be sure.

You could never be sure.

The moonlight gleamed on the white china door handle so that it was like another, smaller moon inside the room and as his eyes closed he remembered the door at Kielty's, which had had no handle at all, saw it, and then other pictures slid and shifted about inside his head. Kielty's.

All their faces, all their eyes, had turned towards

him as he had walked in behind Finn. But they had not looked especially surprised, or even interested. He saw again the sour light in the kitchen and the red-brown eyes of the fox, saw the broken window with one strip of wood nailed across and Dorry Kielty's greasy dark plaits, and a crucifix made out of tin and stuck all over with beads and rose-pink shells, hanging on the wall above the range. Then he went spinning down into sleep, hearing Kielty's voice muttering to the fox and the scrape-scrape of a knife peeling potatoes and the gritting of a cat's teeth as it ate a mouse out on the step.

'Mouse-pie and potatoes, Kielty's eat.'

He had expected to be frightened by them and their strangeness but he was not, had wondered what terrible secret he would discover but there had been none. Racing back, past the windmill and down the hill he had said, I like it there, I like Kielty's, and then was filled with shame and prayed, half-aloud, that he would never admit it to anyone, not even by chance. Though he could not have told why.

'They can't find out.'

The moonlight spread out across the whole door and the rose-patterned wall and Jed slept and by morning, the memory of his visit to Kielty's was pushed deep down and forgotten because today was the journey. The holiday. Todley.

It was joy. The greatest joy he knew. From the moment

when he smelled the smoke under the great ribbed roof of the station he was half way to the city – to him, train smoke and the grime on the carriage windows were city smoke, city grime.

But for a long time he still saw only country, only green, green and sometimes the yellow of corn and straw, sometimes the brown of turned earth, for a long time he looked out and was bored by it all. He thought, go on, go on and pumped his legs to and fro trying to push the train forwards and faster as if he were riding a horse.

'You've everything to be grateful for,' they had always said, Aunt Hatt and Uncle Wilf and Ganty, who was too old and crippled to leave her chair now and only had a view across the street, to the other dark houses, and Stanley who helped in the butcher's shop. 'A country boy. Fresh air, fresh food, animals and plants, everything open and clean. It's what your Da worked for and there's plenty would envy you.'

'Why? *Why?*' It was the city that he liked and the beauty of back alleys and redded steps and the lights from the brickworks at night, flaring like the devil's pit out of the sky.

'Why?'

They shook their heads at him, never understanding.

They ate cold meat sandwiches and slices of apple pie with cheese and the train stopped at Milham Market where Da took his sheep and pigs and then on and on through the still familiar, still hated, still grass-green world.

But then, the uneasiness which lay like a vapour in his mind over the whole of Todley thickened so that he could not tell if it made the excitement, the agitated longing, worse or better. Fear. It always began as they passed the slaughterhouse sheds at Milham and he thought of the beasts. Because how could he tell if their own sheep, which he had often seen born, their own piglets, did not go from Milham to arrive, dead and with dried blood clotted on nostrils and feet, at Uncle Wilf's shop? Where there were knives and choppers and axes with blades keen as ice, skewers and hooks and sausage and mincing machines which Stanley pretended would come alive and trap Jed's fingers. Stanley's own fingers were fat and round and smooth as sausages, blue-tinged even in summer. And behind the huge white door lay the terrible room. 'Cold as death,' Stanley said. The refrigerated room. It was full of death too, though it was not death you could smell, like you smelled it sweet and warm and raw at Milham Market. The terrible room was full of skinned animals, veined like marble, hanging upside down from hooks.

One year, joking, 'trying him for nerve', Uncle Wilf and Stanley had shut Jed inside the refrigerated room. Only for a moment and they had not bolted the door. But it was long enough. Jed had closed his eyes and put

out a hand to touch the cold feathers of a dead cocker-
el for comfort.

Ma had been born and bred in Todley and would
never have set foot back there after her escape if it had
not been for family, for Ganty and her brother.
Though she did not feel close to them, had not done
so since Uncle Wilf's first wife Lois, Ma's best friend,
from school, had died. Now there was the new aunt
and none of them had ever taken to her; they said Aunt
Hatt had a peculiar mind, odd ways, weird friends.
And though she had always been kind to Jed and kept
a box of violet creams in a drawer just for him, he knew
what they meant. He did not like the smell of her.

Todley. Fear. Danger even. You could never be
sure.

But now the train was slowing down, passing the
blue-black slag heaps, the smoke from all the chimneys
was spreading out over their heads and the soft soot
fell. It was joy.

Nor, for three days, did anything happen to change it
and sights and sounds and smells that used to make
him fearful and loomed towards him, monstrous,
through his sleep, seemed ordinary and acceptable. He
walked slowly into the butcher's shop and stood looking at slippery offal and shell-pink brawn, a bucket full
of blood clots for the black puddings, he felt the saw-
dust under his feet, and realised for the first time that
he saw worse things almost every day at home. For the

country held violence and pain and casual cruelty, among animals and among men, and he passed it by or mingled with it as he got on with his own life. Last week Barker's cow had tried to jump a ditch as she was calving and landed straddle across the spiked fence on her belly, died as they were trying to hack her free or haul her off. There were traps and guns in the woods, his father's hands wringing the necks of turkeys and setting the ferrets down rabbit holes, the dogs after hares. So that when Uncle Wilf told him to lay his hand, palm upwards, on the wooden chopping block and then raised the meat axe high and swung it down, laughing, to within an inch of his fingers, Jed had not flinched, only stared up at the man's ox-red face, unblinking, unafraid.

'He's comin' on,' Uncle Wilf said, and gave him a shilling out of the till. 'Comin' on.'

Jed had trousered the money and gone to stand in the street to watch the trams and his head rang with happiness at their noise and with pride in himself and his own courage. 'Comin' on.' He touched a hand to his hair and it came away smeared with coal grit, and that made for joy later as he looked down at the curded scum around the washbasin, seeing how different this dirt was from what Ma called the 'clean dirt' at home. There dirt came in brown clods, wet and meal, dirt was earth or dung or leaf mould. Todley dirt was real. He pictured it filtering through the pores of his skin and settling inside him forever.

'They die of dirt,' Ma said, 'Todley folk. Choke all the way to their graves on it. You think yourself lucky.'

But he did not.

And still nothing happened. But it seemed to Jed that things had somehow changed in the narrow house. Less daylight strained into the front parlour where Ganty sat and she herself was smaller, as though her limbs had folded in upon themselves. There was no space to move about between chairs and tables and sideboards and cupboards and cabinets, all the rooms were like mouths over-packed with dark stained teeth.

'Don't be daft, it's you. Grown, haven't you?'

Yes. They had not been here for two years. 'Grown.'

Though Stanley and Uncle Wilf were still giants.

Nothing happened. He said 'Todley' to himself over and over, scarcely believing he was here. 'Todley.'

Joy.

Until Thursday night.

'There's people coming in. Friends of your Aunt Hatt.' Though Ma had not sounded as if she meant 'friends' as she had folded the top sheet tight beneath his chin. 'So mind you get to sleep.'

'I want to see them. Why can't I?'

He wanted to see Todley folk, friends or not, they were magic and mystery to him, as people who lived in different countries and whose unfamiliar ways made their mark upon the set and texture of their faces, the strange movements of their hands and eyes. He noticed how quickly Todley people walked and with their heads bent down so that he rarely saw their eyes and could not tell what they were thinking. At home everyone went slowly, to a rhythm, and looking all about them like Da had taught him, because that way you learned what was vital to you, from the shape and depth of shadows over the hills, the way the animals were pressed up close together or scattered about, anxious or quiet, under the trees and hedges or in the open, to east or to west. At home everything was measured and, to those that knew, predictable. Here nothing was, except for the sound of the blowers from pit and brickworks marking the beginnings and ends of the shifts.

He sat up in bed.

'I could come down for cocoa.' And Aunt Hatt's violet scented chocolates. Once, they had given him two or three sips from a glass of sherry and his eyes had swerved about. Everyone had laughed. He remembered that.

'Just for a bit. They'd not mind. The friends.'

'You could get off to sleep. There's no one to interest you.'

'Who are they then?'

'Just people.'

And she raked the marigold curtains across the rail and that was the end of it, though the bedroom was never dark because of the brickworks and the wax-yellow street lamps and the lights from the night trams moving in segments like luminous caterpillars over the ceiling. Todley was never dark, never silent.

He could stay awake, watch the lights, count the trams, until he heard the visitors come. Then go down.

He slept.

Woke. Thought, now it is night. Because at first, when he got out of bed and opened his door he could not hear anything. The house was oddly still, tense.

He went a little way, cautiously, down the stairs.

There was a voice, then another, but the voices sounded strange, slow and quiet; it was not the family talking, interrupting each other, laughing over cups of tea or a glass of cider. The light showing beneath the parlour door was different too, dimmer, as though someone had shaded it with a cloth. He had meant to walk straight in, pretending a bad dream or a thirst, knowing they would welcome him, even Ma, spoil him with chocolates as though he were still only four years old, sensing that his appearance provided them with some relief from the tedium of one another's company in the close, crammed room.

But something was not right. Jed sat down on the bottom step. The voice began again, murmuring, making him drowsy. Then, a clink, like the touch of a spoon on a glass. He leaned forwards trying to hear and at the same time wrapped his arms around his knees and clasped his hands tightly together for reassurance. The light under the door shifted from one side to the other slowly, as though someone had moved a lamp. His eyes closed again. Perhaps after all there was no one there, they had damped down the fire and gone to bed and he himself was in bed too, still sleeping, dreaming. But he moved and felt the metal treads of the carpet, cold and hard against his thigh. He slid off the stair and crouched, paused and then moved forwards, stealthy and secret as a poacher in Thwaites wood, as close to the door as he dared.

Go in. Go in.

No.

Someone was spelling out words very slowly and uncertainly, as he had done when he was learning to read.

'F… No. Yes. F-F…O.' Aunt Hatt's voice. 'F…O… what are you trying to tell me? Is it a name? F… no, N… N…O. No. Not a name. F… Someone's pushing the glass. Wilf.'

'I've not touched it.'

'It's coming now.. It's F.. F..O…X. Fox? Yes, fox.'

Was it a game? Jed leaned into the keyhole. He could just see the edge of the table, covered in a moss-green cloth. Aunt Hatt sometimes told fortunes from cards but he could see none tonight. The old paraffin lamp was lit and it threw up a peculiar, dusky glow onto Aunt Hatt's face and made shadows like pits where her eyes and lips should be.

'Fox?'

'It's mother !'

'Now then..'

'Be quiet Wilf.' She leaned forwards blocking out the light and that made Jed feel safer. He had not liked to see the expression on her face.

'It's mother, it's mothers fox fur. I've kept it all these years, she did love it so. She's telling me. She knew it's what I'd recognise isn't it?Mother?'

'There was a lad I once knew.. Foxy Blackett.'

'No, no, it's mother I've told you, I've got a feeling for it. A sense. Mother? I'm here I'm listening. Move the glass, move the glass. You're not to worry about the fur. I've got it safe. I'd never part with that.'

'Foxy Hackett, not Blackett. I remember now. Frank his real name was. House on the corner of Arden Street. You'll remember him Nelly?'

Ma did not reply.

'Got a direct hit. 1942. Foxy Hackett.'

'Move the glass again mother, I'm here, I'm waiting.'

'It's stopped now.'

'Something's wrong, something's upset her. There's a different feeling in the room. Oh that fox fur, she loved it, I know you loved it mother. She always said it made her feel like a lady.'

'Nothing's started and nothing's stopped,' Uncle Wilf said. 'Don't get worked up over it, I've told you before. It's a bit of fun.'

'She was with us, it's as clear as day. Clear to me. I knew it. Fox.'

Fox. Terror spurted up from deep inside Jed and burned through him, Because now he knew what they were doing and that it was not a game. He had heard Ma talking about it to her brother.

'Wicked,' she'd said, 'the devil's work.'

He had laughed and said she was to take no notice, it was a bit of fun, it was only Hatt who wanted to believe in it, like the cards and the tea-leaves and the Friday night meetings at Miss Myrtle's.

'Where's the harm? It's all stuff, you know it, I know it, but it keeps her happy.'

'Happy? There's some things best left.'

'Leave her be and keep your thoughts to yourself. Haven't I learned to do that? It does no harm.'

'It does no good either. Let the past bury its dead.'

But it was not dead people, not tonight, Jed knew that. It was far worse than dead people. He did not believe they could hurt you. But Ma had said nothing often enough.

'Truth will out.'

Fox.

He wanted to get away from the door and back up the stairs, to stuff his head deep under the blankets, hide and then pray for there to be no more truths spelled out by the glass.

'It's moving again. Someone else. There's someone else.' Aunt Hatt.

He tried to crawl backwards and could, not move, his legs were too numbed; he remembered the stories of people turned to blocks of stone or salt for punishment.

'Someone else.'

He knew that he had to wait, had to hear.

They got four letters and it took a long time, they were confused by the glass, though Jed could have walked in and told them the whole word. He did not, but only knelt there helplessly until they should open the door and see, looking into his face, see there the secret which was no longer a secret, and the whole wickedness of it.

'K…I….E…'It's stopped again. I don't understand this one. KIE… L.. is that an L? K..I..E…L… Is it a name? Is this your name? Answer yes or no. It won't move. K..I..E..L.'

Jed put the back of his hand up to his mouth ad bit it to stop himself from screaming.

'Kiel? Who is it? Who's Kiel?'

He could not bear it any longer. He managed, somehow, to reach the stairs and pull himself up them and now he was gasping, so they must surely hear him. In his head he lay trembling the pillow clutched tight to him and now, now they would come.

He had been up to Kielty's, he had seen the fox. 'Truth will out.'

He had not believed it but now he knew and there was no hope for him, no possible escape. Nor would Todley ever be joy again.

In the end he stopped trembling and only waited,

stiff and still and cold, hardly breathing. Waited.

In the parlour, it was Miss Clagdon who spoke, Miss Clagdon who was said by those at the Friday meetings to have 'healing hands.'

'The niece.' It was a whisper and she was leaning back in her chair, out of reach of the lamp, so that they would not see her face.

'Niece? We've got no nieces.'

'Mine. Enid's girl. She's not talked of.'

'A tragedy dear?'

Miss Clagdon took out a handkerchief and patted at the sweat that beaded her greyish skin.

'Went off with one of the prisoners of war from Creydale, from the Polish Camp.'

'That long ago?'

'They won't have her name spoken. Got herself into trouble.'

'Forgive and forget. Isn't this your chance? You can help her now. That's right, within families.'

'I tried. She did away with herself in Stackton Canal and the child too. Tied it in a sack.'

Tears came, mingling with the sweat.

'It's past,' Wilf said and his voice boomed in the room, startling them. 'And done with.' He heaved himself up, anxious to have things normal again, put on the lights and stoke up a decent fire. No harm in it, he'd said to Ellen. Still, it brought up too many things that were best forgotten.

But his wife sat on, close to the board, her hand resting on the tumbler, her heart beating too fast, for these were what she sought and fed upon, these secrets and confessions.

She said, 'But if it was her…'

'It was.'

'I don't follow dear. It wasn't a name, was it, I didn't get a name. K..I..E..L.'

'Not a name, a place. The man was a German. She wouldn't give a name, she'd be too ashamed. It was where he came from – Kiel. That's a town in Germany. We knew that and we never knew more, and we never wanted to know. Kiel. He came from Kiel.'

Wilf switched on the lights and in the sudden brightness caught sight of his wife's face and was sickened by the greed upon it and by the sigh of satisfaction that came from her even as she turned to her friend Miss Clagdon, ready with more sympathy.

'There'll not be any more of this nonsense,' he said, 'in future. I'll not have it.'

And meant it. But he knew that there was no point and that he was powerless in his own house.

Upstairs Jed lay. Waited.

Waited for four days and nights, the remainder of their time, afraid to catch his mother's eye or to be alone in a room with Aunt Hatt, and as every hour passed the dread swelled within him so that there seemed to be no room for the food and drink he must swallow and in sleep a hand came over his face and pressed him down until he choked and stifled on the appalling dreams.

But no one spoke of the truths that had been uncovered.

'I'll go to them, tell them, make me punish me now,' he thought. For nothing could be worse than this waiting, this fear of what was to happen. When his mother came into his room each night he opened his mouth, tried to say it, but could not.

'The boy looks peaky.'

'Needs to be home again, that's all. Needs the open air. I told you this is no place for a child. No place for anyone, Todley.'

No. And now he wanted to be away, to be home, he could not imagine how Todley had ever been joy. Todley was darkness and misery and sulphurous flames and stench. He blocked out the noises from the brick-work and the steelyard and the pithead and the trams but, like the soot beneath his skin they had forced their way into him now and rang and chopped and crashed and clanged without ceasing to the rhythm of his blood. God let it be over. God let Monday come.

It came. He lay back against the seat of the train compartment and pretended to sleep, counted up to three thousand very slowly and when he opened his eyes saw that everything was green again, and wept.

'What's that for? There'll be another year won't there? Todley's like the poor, always there, never doing anyone any good and if you knew it as long as I have you'd not cry at leaving, you'd cry at the thought of going back.'

Jed stared at her. She knew, she *knew* , so why was she pretending to him, why had she still said nothing?

He was waiting to tell Da. Da was the one who'd do the punishing. But there was no more fear left in him, he was weary of it and weak with it so that whatever Da said or did could only be a relief.

'Milham Market.'

The sun was like a golden fan spread out over the cornfields and when the wind blew the fan slid together, opened out again. The shadows cast by barns and hayricks were like violet bruises. He thought, it is beautiful after all and it is good. The devil can't follow here. The sun shone onto his face through the train window.

He knelt on the rag rug before the fire, twisting bits of the cloth around his finger, and the milk was warm and sticky as it slipped down his throat, soothing away the very last of his fear. He had been anxious when they had first got back and gone everywhere about the place, walking cautiously, unlatching the doors of stables and sheds and sties, smelling the warm acrid smells of cattle, touching the backs of the pigs. *You could never be sure.* But he was. He had looked across at the fields, up at the sky and right into the face of the moon.

Home.

'You think yourself lucky, boy,' He did. Though he touched the wood of the fence all the same.

'Five more minutes.'

Da had been telling them about the storm four nights ago, the worst for years, with thunderclaps to wake the dead. 'All hell let loose,' he said. He'd been up half the night, fastening things down, calming the animals. Even Rector Pickering's father who was ninety eight years old had never known a storm like it. Half the land belonging to those who farmed lower down, on the other side of the river, had been flooded and was still. Ted Gomersall had lost fourteen cows.

'And then't crops. Crops fared worst.'

But they were sheep and dairy mostly and counted their blessings.

Jed looked into the fire and saw pictures between his half-closed eyes and hardly listened, hardly thought, except for wishing that he had been here during the great storm instead of at Todley, for then he might have been up and outside with Da, helping.

The fire was pear-tree logs from Rector Pickering's old orchard and burned even and sweet and slow.

'Kielty's went,' Da said.

Jed's fingers tightened on the rug.

'Before first light. Piled themselves into that truck and off, took whatever wasn't nailed down and some of that an all.'

'With no one to help?'

'Didn't ask, and who'd have offered?'

'On a night like that and after what they'd suffered? Anyone would. It's be common charity.'

'There was enough else to see to.'

'I'd have done something, never mind what you thought.'

'I said, they'd neither ask nor accept. They knew where they stood, Kielty's.'

One of the logs shifted, disintegrated into the hearth like chalk, startling Jed so that he sat up and looked at them. He had been half-drowsing, half-day-dreaming and so he had missed what was important.

'What? What happened to Kieltys?'

'Bed for you.'

'What happened?'

'Boiling your brains in front of t'fire. You'll have bad dreams.'

'Scorch himself more like.'

'*What?*

'To Kielty's? They went. I said.'

'You were saying about the storm.'

'That was it. Lightning struck the old windmill first and set it on fire and then next minute Kielty's roof. Went up like a tinder-box.'

That fire, and the lightning and the burning logs and the flames from Todley brickworks and the paraffin lamp in the parlour and all the fires in the world, blazed up through him. He said, 'Kieltys are dead and burned up.' And began to scream.

After that it made no difference what they said. He did not care because he knew the truth and there was no help or comfort and never would be, He told them over and over again why Kieltys were dead, that it was the work of the devil, who could reach as far as here after all, reach him; it was his punishment.

Ma had given him something hot and bitter to drink and he wanted to throw it up because that tasted of fire too.

'They've gone. What's to bother about?'

'Kieltys are dead.'

'Nobody's dead. Where'd you get that idea? They took what they could and left and good riddance. People like Kieltys will always fare.'

Jed tried to struggle against the press of sleep, reared up, pushing back the sheets.

'Dead.'

Da touched a finger, rough as grain, to Jed's face.

'All that was found dead,' he said, 'was a beast. One.'

He lay back then, gave in and only looked into Da's face and waited.

'One fox.'

He went down then, falling, falling into the devil's pit.

MR PROUDHAM AND MR SLEIGHT

That evening, I saw Mr Proudham and Mr Sleight for the first time. I had set out to walk all the way along the sea front but the sleet and a north-easterly wind soon drove me back to the tall, Edwardian house in which I had rented a flat. I had chosen to come here at the bleakest time of year, partly because I gained an obscure satisfaction from physical endurance. But mainly because nobody would trouble me. The flat had no telephone.

The sky was gunmetal grey. Only two or three other people had ventured out, women briskly walking their dogs. They wore long tweed coats padded out with cardigans underneath and sensible, sheepskin-lined boots and scarves wound round their heads for the protection of mouths and ears. Nobody looked at me.

But when I opened the front gate of the house Mr Proudham and Mr Sleight were looking. It was almost dark and they had not put the light on in their ground floor window. They stood side by side, shadowy, improbably figures. I was to see the like that so often during the weeks to come – Mr Proudham,

immensely tall and etiolated, with a thin head and
unhealthy, yellowish skin: and Mr Sleight, perhaps five
feet one or two, with a benevolent, rather stupid moon
of a face. He was bald: Mr Proudham had dingy-white
hair, worn rather long.

I hesitated, fiddling with the latch. They stood,
watching. They made no secret of their curiosity, they
had no net curtain behind which they might hide. But
their faces were curiously expressionless. The sleet had
turned to hail. I went quickly inside. Mr Proudham
and Mr Sleight continued to watch me until I had
passed out of sight, under the shadow of the porch.

It was a full week before they introduced themselves
– or rather, before Mr Proudham introduced them, for
little Mr Sleight nodded and beamed and clicked his
false teeth but rarely spoke. When he did, it was to
murmur with his friend.

Each time I left the house they were watching me.
And I began, a little more surreptitiously, to watch
them. They had a dog, an overgrown sooty poodle
which was clipped in not quite the usual fashion, but
in horizontal bands going round its body and up the
tail, so that from a distance it appeared to be striped in
two-tone grey. Mr Proudham always held the lead and
Mr Slight trotted alongside keeping time with the dog.

They went out three times a day, at ten, at two and
at six. In addition, Mr Proudham went out at eleven
each morning carrying a shopping bag of drab olive
cloth. And it was in a shop, Cox's Mini-Market, that I

first came face to face with him. He was buying parsnips and because I was standing at the back of the queue I had a chance to study him. He was considerably older than I had at first thought, with heavy-lidded eyes that drooped at the corners and a mouth very full of teeth. On top of the off-white hair he wore a curious woollen beret, rather like that of a French onion-seller but with a pompom on the top. As he turned to leave the shop he saw me. He stopped. Then, as though he had considered the situation carefully, he bowed, and lifted his hand. For a moment I wondered if he were going to raise the little woollen hat. But he only gave a half-salute.

'Good morning.'

But that time he did not reply.

Later, I was working at my desk in the window when I saw the two of them go off down the path for their two o'clock walk. It was one of those lowering, east coast days which had never come fully light. Both men wore long knitted scarves in bright multi-colours, which hung down their backs like those of children or students. But only Mr Proudham had a hat – the woolly beret. They did not seem in the least disconcerted that I was sitting there, looking back at them. For what can only have been ten seconds but felt considerably longer they stood, so that I almost waved, to prevent embarrassment. But I did not, and eventually they moved off on their walk.

That evening, Mr Proudham spoke. I had been out

to post a letter. The temperature had dropped again, so that my breath smoked on the air and the sea was glistening with reflected frost. It was quite dark. As I came up the alleyway between two houses, which led from the High Street on to the sea front, I saw them a few yards away. The dog was sniffing busily around the concrete bollard. Some decision must have been reached by them earlier for, as though they had been waiting for this moment, Mr Proudham stepped forward to meet me.

'I am Mr Proudham, this is Mr Sleight. How do you do?'

It was a formal little speech. He had a rather high-pitched voice, and I saw that there were even more teeth than I had first noticed, long and crowded together. We shook hands and the dog turned its attention from the bollard and began to sniff me.

'We do hope you are comfortable at number forty-three? We do hope you have everything you require?'

Yes, I said, I was very comfortable. And I looked at Mr Sleight, who at once blushed and glanced at Mr Proudham, and then away, and then down at the dog. He did not speak, though I thought that the movement of his mouth indicated that he might wish to.

'We do hope you were not expecting better weather. Alas, it is never better than this in late November.'

I told him it was what I had been prepared for.

'Yes. I see, I see, I see.'

Then abruptly he pulled at the dog's lead and

touched the arm of Mr Sleight. Mr Sleight jumped and his eyes began to swivel about again. He was smiling into space.

'I'm afraid there is not much entertainment here,' Mr Proudham said. They were already moving off, so that when he repeated the sentence, his words were carried away down the sea front on the wind.

'No entertainment…'

'Goodbye.' But they were already out of earshot. I looked back at them, the tall, thin figure and the short round one with the brightly coloured scarves hanging like pigtails down behind. The striped dog was pulling at the end of the lead, so that Mr Proudham had to bend forward. I smiled. But there was something about them that was not altogether funny.

At the front door I looked for their names above the bell. 'Proudham and Sleight' were written, like a firm of solicitors. No initials. Proudham and Sleight.

I drew my curtains and switched on the electric fire. I would work for another couple of hours before supper. A little later, I heard them come in, heard doors open and close gently. They were very quiet. Mr Proudham and Mr Sleight, they did not seem to have a television or wireless set, or to shout to one another from room to room, as is sometimes the habit of those who live together. Most of the time, there might have been no one at all in the flat below.

I had gone there to work undisturbed, but I also spent a good time walking, either along the beach itself for several miles or on the promenade which followed the shore from the south side, where I was living, right up to the breakwater at the most northerly point of the town. It was here that a few amusements were situated. Most of them were closed at this time of year but I liked to wander past the canvas-shrouded dodgem hall, the blank lights and peeling paint. There was an open air swimming pool, drained for the winter, and sand and silt had been washed over the rim by the storm tides. Near to this was a café and one amusement centre, called Gala Land, both of which remained open.

I could not keep away from Gala Land. It had a particular smell which drew me down the steep flight of concrete steps to the pay desk below. It was built underground in a sort of valley between two outcrops of rock, over which was a ribbed glass roof, like those of Victorian railway stations and conservatories. The walls were covered in greenish moss and the whole place had a close, damp, musty smell and although it was lit from end to end with neon and fluorescent lights, everything looked somehow dark, furtive and gone to seed. Some of the booths were closed down here, too, and those which kept open must have lost money, except perhaps on the few days when parties of trippers came from inland, in the teeth of the weather, and dived down for shelter to the underground fun palace. Then, for a few hours, the fruit and try-your-strength and fortune card machines whirred, loud cracks echoed from the rifle ranges, hurdy-gurdy music sounded out, there was a show of gaiety. For the rest of the time the place was mainly patronized by a few unemployed men and teenage boys, who chewed gum and fired endless rounds of blank ammunition at the bobbing rows of duck targets, and by older school-children after four o'clock. At the far end was a roller skating rink which drew a good crowd on Saturday afternoons.

I liked that sad, shabby place, I liked its atmos-phere. Occasionally I put a coin into a fruit machine or watched What the Butler Saw. There was a more grue-some peepshow, too, in which one could watch a con-demned man being led on to a platform, hooded and noosed and then dropped snap, down through a trap-door to death. I watched this so often that, long after I had left the town, this scene featured in my night-mares, I smelled the brackish, underground smell.

It was in Gala Land, early one Thursday afternoon, that I saw Mr Proudham. He was alone, and operating one of the football machines. A dropped coin set a small ball rolling among a set of figures which could be swivelled from side to side by means of a lever. The aim was to make one of them bang the ball into the goal before it rolled out of sight down a slot in the side. Mr Proudham was concentrating hard, bending over the machine and manipulating the handles with great energy. He wore, as usual, the woolly pompom hat and a grey mackintosh. I watched him as he had three tries and then succeeded in knocking the ball into a goal with the fourth. He stood upright and retrieved his coin from the metal dish.

'Well done!' I said.

He turned, and for a moment I thought he was going to scuttle away, pretending that he had not recognized me. Instead he smiled, showing all those teeth. I would have asked if he came here often. But at once, he said, 'Today is Mr Sleight's day at the clinic. I always come down here to pass the time you know, until he is due to return. I have somehow to pass the time.'

I hoped that Mr Sleight was not seriously ill. Mr Proudham leaned forward a little, lowering his voice. 'It's the massage, you see. He goes for the massage.'

I did not like to enquire further, and I would have made some excuse to leave quickly then, in case Mr Proudham felt embarrassed at being caught in Gala Land. But he asked, with a rather strange, cat-like expression on his face, if I would care for some tea.

'There is quite a *clean* cafe, just beside the pool, they do make a very reasonable cup of tea. I generally go there on Mr Sleight's day at the clinic. It passes the time. I like to give myself something to do. Yes.'

And so he escorted me out of the damp-smelling, half-empty funfair and up to the ground level, where Timpson's Seagull Café was also half-empty, and smelled of china tiles and urn-tea.

I did not know what I might talk to Mr Proudham about, over our pot of tea, but I need not have worried because, as though he wanted to deflect any attention from himself, he began to ask me questions, about my work, my life in London, London itself. They were not personal, probing questions – I could answer them in detail and yet not give much away. Mr Proudham listened, smiling every now and again with all those teeth. He was the one who poured out the tea. I noticed that his eyes were bloodshot and that the yellowish cheeks were shot through here and there with broken veins. How old was he? Seventy? Perhaps not quite, or perhaps a year or two more, it was hard to tell.

Suddenly he said, 'Behind you is a photograph of my mother.' I looked around.

The picture was an old one, in an oak frame, of the grandstand which had been demolished during the last war. There were flowers, mostly hydrangeas, banked around the base and awnings draped above, hung with tassels. Sitting in the bandstand was a Ladies Orchestra. There were all dressed in white, Grecian style garments, hanging in folds to the floor, with floral headbands. They looked wide-eyed, vacant and curiously depressed.

'My mother,' said Mr Proudham, 'is the Lady Conductor.'

And there she was, a large-bosomed woman with wildly curling hair, who clutched her baton like a fairy's wand.

I said, how interesting.

'She died in 1937,' Mr Proudham said. 'I myself was never musical. It was her great sadness.'

'So you have always lived here.'

Mr Proudham inclined his head. Then, as if he were afraid of having given too much away, he looked up brightly, clapping his hands together.

'Now – I hope you are not a believer in blood sports.'

We stayed in Timpson's Seagull Café until just before five o'clock, when he jumped up and began to pull on gloves and wind his scarf anxiously, for Mr Sleight would be home from the clinic.

'And I make a point of being in,' Mr Proudham said, 'I think that is so important, don't you? To be in. I am always waiting.'

He shook hands with me, across the green formica table, as though one of us were departing on a journey, and rushed away.

After that I saw them together most days, and Mr Proudham always spoke and Mr Sleight smiled and looked nervous, and once or twice I bumped into Mr Proudham alone. But Mr Sleight was never alone. I wondered if he might be a little simple, unable to cope with the outside world by himself. On Thursday afternoons a taxi drew up and he went off in it to 'the clinic'. Mr Proudham left the house shortly after, to walk in the direction of the funfair and the Seagull Café.

The week before Christmas they issued an invitation. I had been for a walk along the beach, in the snow, and when I returned there was an envelope pushed underneath my door.

*

Would you care to take tea with us on Saturday next? Unless we hear to the contrary, we greatly look forward to seeing you at 4.30 p.m.

The note was written in a neat, rather childish hand on cream paper. I replied to it, putting my own card underneath the door while they were out on their six o'clock walk. For I wanted to satisfy my curiosity about them. I wanted to see inside their flat. And I felt rather sorry for them, a pair of elderly men who never had a visitor.

On that Saturday morning, Mr Proudham went out alone not once but twice and returned each time with a full shopping bag. I put on a red dress, and wished that I had some gift I could take with me.

Mr Proudham opened the door. He was wearing a canary yellow waistcoat, over a boldly checked shirt and matching cravat. In the sitting room I found Mr Sleight with his bald head almost invisible over the polo neck of a bright orange jumper. We made a highly-coloured trio standing uncertainly together in the centre of the room, which was stiflingly hot, with a log fire and three radiators turned on to full. 'Now please sit down, please sit down.' I picked a chair well away from the hearth and, for a moment, Mr Proudham and Mr Sleight both stood over me, their faces beaming proudly. Perhaps no one had been here to tea before.

When Mr Proudham did speak, it was a little 'Ah!'

like a sigh of satisfaction, as though he were a photographer who had arranged a perfect tableau. 'Ah!' and he glanced at Mr Sleight and nodded and smiled and held out a hand in my direction. Mr Sleight smiled. I smiled. The hot room was full of bonhomie.

They might have been expecting a party of schoolboys for tea. There was white and brown bread and butter, muffins, toast, gentleman's relish, honey, crab apple jelly, fruit loaf, fruit cake, chocolate gateau, éclairs, meringues, shortbread fingers. I ate as much as I could, but Mr Proudham and Mr Sleight ate a good deal more, cake after cake, and drank cups of sugary tea. Conversation lapsed. The poodle dog watched from the other side of the room. I wondered how we would get through the time after tea, and whether Mr Sleight were dumb.

They had bought or inherited some beautiful furniture – a set of Chippendale chairs, a Jacobean oak table, a dresser hung with Crown Derby china. The carpet was Persian, there were Cotman and Birkett Foster watercolours on the walls. And in an alcove near the window stood an enormous tropical fish tank. In another corner, a parrot in a cage sat so perfectly still and silent I thought it might be a dummy.

Eventually, Mr Proudham wiped crumbs of meringue from around his mouth with a purple handkerchief. He said, 'I think that Mr Sleight has something to *show* you.' It was the tone a mother would use about her child which has some drawing or piece of handiwork to proffer. Mr Sleight gave a little, nervous cough.

I could not have been in the least prepared for what I was to see. Mr Sleight led me, with a slightly flustered air, out of the room and down a short passage, and through a heavily beaded curtain which he held aside for me, and which rattled softly as he let it go. Mr Proudham stood well back.

'Now this is Mr Sleight's territory. I never interfere. This is *all* his own.'

It was rather dark, apart from two spotlights attached to the wall above a long workbench. Shelves had been fitted all round the room, and displayed on the shelves, as well as on the window-ledge and several small tables, were rows of wax-work models. They were a little larger than children's puppets, and similarly grotesque, but a good deal more carefully made.

Mr Sleight stood back, his eyes flicking here and there about the room, occasionally resting on me for a second, as he tried to judge what I was thinking. I stepped closer to the bench and looked down at the two models which were in progress, at enamel bowls of wax, rubber moulds and papier-mâché bases, and small chisels and blades and neat little piles of hair. And, looking round, I saw the faces of Mr Proudham and Mr Sleight, smiling and motionless lie two, larger wax-works, dressed in those startling colours.

THE CUSTODIAN

At five minutes to three he climbed up the ladder into the loft. He went cautiously. He was always cautious now moving his limbs warily and never going out in bad weather without enough warm clothes. For the truth was that he had not been expected to survive this winter. He was old. He had been ill for a week and then the fear had come over him that he was going to die. He did not care for himself, but what would become of the boy? It was only the boy he worried about now, only the boy who mattered. So he was careful with himself. He had lived out this bad winter and now it was March, he could look forward to the spring and summer, cease to worry for a while longer. All the same, he had to be careful not to have accidents, though he was steady enough on his feet. He was seventy one. He knew how easy it would be to miss his footing on this narrow ladder, to break a limb and lie there while all the time the child waited, panic welling up in him, left last at the school gate. And when the fear of the consequences of his own dying did not grip him he was haunted by ideas of some long illness or incapacity; if he had to be taken to hospital what would happen to the child then? *What would happen?*

But now it was almost three o'clock, almost time for him to leave the house, his favourite part of the day, now he climbed onto his hands and knees into the cool, dim loft and felt about among the apples, holding this one and that one up to the light sifting through the roof slats, wanting the fruit he eventually chose to be perfectly ripe, perfectly smooth.

The loft smelled sweetly of the apples and pears laid up there since the previous autumn. Above his head he heard the scrabbling noises of the birds that nested in the eaves and his heart flipped with joy that it was almost April, almost spring.

He went carefully back down the ladder, holding the chosen apple. It took him twenty minutes to walk to the school but he liked to arrive early, to have the pleasure of watching and waiting outside the gates.

The sky was brittle blue and the sun shone but it was very cold, the air still smelled of winter. Until a fortnight before there had been snow, he and the boy had trudged back and forth every morning and afternoon over the frost-hard paths leading across the marshes and the stream running alongside them had been iced over, the reeds were stiff and white as blades.

It had thawed only gradually. Today, the air smelled

thin and sharp in his nostrils. Nothing moved. As he climbed the grass bank onto the higher path he looked across at the great stretch of river gleaming like a metal plate under the winter sun, still as the sky. Everything was pale, white and silver; a gull flew over and the undersides of its wings were silver grey. There were no sounds here except the sudden chatter of dunlin swooping and dropping quickly down, and the tread of his own feet on the path, the brush of his legs against the stiff grass clumps.

He had not expected to see the end of this winter.

In his hand he felt the apple, soothing to his touch. The boy must have fruit every day, he saw to that, as well as eggs and milk which they fetched from Maldrun's farm a mile away. His limbs should grow straight and strong. He should be perfect.

Maldrun's cattle were out, on their green island in the middle of the marshes surrounded by the moat of steely water; he led them across a narrow path like a causeway from the farm. They were like toy animals, or ones in a picture, from this distance away, they stood motionless, cut out shapes of black and white. Every so often the boy would be afraid of going past the island of cows. He gripped the old man's hand and a tight expression came over his face.

'They can't get to you, don't you see? They don't cross water, cows, they hate water. They're not bothered about you.'

'I know.'

He did know and was still afraid, though there had been days recently when he would go right up to the edge of the strip of water and stare across at the animals and would even accompany Maldrun to the half-door of the milking parlour, climb up and look over, would smell the thick, warm, sweet-sour cow smell and hear the splash of pats onto the stone floor. The cows had great bony haunches and soft eyes.

'Touch one,' Maldrun had said. The boy had gone inside and put out a hand, though still standing well back, stroked the rough pelt, and the cow had twitched feeling the lightness of his hand as if it were an irritation, the prick of a fly. He was afraid of the cows but getting less so. So many things were changing. He was growing. He was eight years old.

Occasionally the old man woke in the night and sweated with fear that he might die before the boy was grown up and he prayed then that he would live ten more years, just ten, until he could look after himself. And some days it seemed possible, seemed, indeed, more than likely, some days he felt very young, felt no age at all, his arms were strong, he could chop wood and lift buckets; he became light-headed with the sense of his own youth.

He was no age at all. He was seventy one, a tall, bony man with thick white hair and without any spread of spare flesh. When he bathed he looked down and saw every rib, every joint of his own thin body, bent an arm and watched the flicker of muscle beneath the skin.

As the path curved round the sun caught the surface of the water on his right so that it shimmered and dazzled his eyes for a moment, and then he heard the familiar, faint high moan of the wind as it blew off the estuary. The reeds rustled dryly together. He put up the collar of his coat. But he was happy, his own happiness sang inside his head, that he was here, walking along this marsh path with the apple inside his hand inside his pocket, that he would wait and watch and then would walk back again the same way, with the boy, and that none of those things he dreaded had come about.

Looking back he could still make out the shapes of the cows and looking down to where the water lay between the reed-banks he saw a swan, its neck arched and its head below the surface of the dark and glistening stream and it, too, was entirely still. He stopped for a moment watching it and hearing the thin sound of the wind and then, turning, saw the whole, pale stretch of marsh and water and sky, saw for miles, back to where the trees began, behind which was the cottage, and then far ahead to where the sand stretched out like a tongue to the mouth of the estuary.

He was amazed, that he could be alive and moving, small as an insect across this great, bright, cold space, amazed that in this landscape he should count for as much as Maldrun's cows and the unmoving swan.

The wind was cold in his face. It was a quarter past three. He left the path, went towards the gate and began to cross the field which led to the lane. Beyond that it was another mile to the village and the school.

Occasionally he came here not only in the morning and back again in the afternoon but at other times when he was suddenly overcome with anxiety to see the boy, to reassure himself that he was still there, still alive. Then he put down whatever he was doing and came half at a run, stumbling until he reached the railings and the closed black gate. If he waited there long enough, if it was break or dinner time, he saw them all come tumbling out through the green painted doors, watched desperately until he saw him and then his grip on the railings loosened. Always, the boy would come straight to him, running over the asphalt, and laughed and called and pressed himself up against the railings on the other side.

'Hello.'

'All right?'

'What have you brought me? Have you got something?'

But he knew there would be nothing and did not expect it. There would only be the fruit at home-time, apple or pear and sometimes in summer cherries or a peach.

'I was passing through the village.'

'Were you getting the shopping?'

'Yes.'

'We've done reading. We had rice and jam for pudding.'

'That's good. Always eat your dinner.'

'You won't forget to come back will you?'

'Have I ever?'

Then he made himself straighten up. 'You go back to your friends now.'

'You will come, you will be here?'

'I'll be here.'

He turned away. They both turned, for they were separate, they should have their own ways, their own lives. He would walk off down the lane and not allow himself to glance back, calm again, no longer anxious.

He did not mind all the walking even in the worst weather. He did not mind anything at all in this life he had chosen and which was so all-absorbing, the details of which were so important. He no longer thought about the past. Somewhere, he had read that an old man has only his memories and had wondered at it, for he had none – or rather, those he had never concerned him, they were like old letters which he had not bothered to keep. He had, simply, the present; the cottage, the land, and the boy and all of them to look after. And himself. He had to stay well and must not die yet. That was all.

But he did not often allow himself to go up to the school like that at unnecessary times, he would force himself to stay and sweat out his need to see the child and reassure himself in some physical job, he would beat mats and plant vegetables, cut wood, prune, pick fruit or walk over to see Maldrun at the farm, buy a chicken or eggs and wait until the time came slowly round to three o'clock and then he could go, allow himself the pleasure of getting there a little early and waiting beside the open gates for the boy to come out.

'What have I got?'

'You guess.'

'Pear.'

'Wrong !' He opened his hand to reveal the apple.

'I like apples best anyway.'

'I know. I had a good look at those trees down the bottom this morning. There won't be so many this year. They'll be taking a year off.'

'Last year there were hundreds. Thousands.'

He took the old man's hand as they reached the end of the lane. For some reason he always waited until here, just by the whitebeam, before doing that.

'*Millions* of apples.'

'Get on.'

'Well, a lot.'

'You don't get two crops like that in a row.'

'Why don't you?'

'Trees wear themselves out fruiting like that. Need a rest.'

'Will we have a lot of pears instead then?'

'Might do. What have you learned today?'

'Lots of things. Millions of things.'

'Have you learned your reading? That's what's important, you know that, to keep up with reading.'

He had started the boy off himself, bought an alphabet book from the shop in the village and when they had got beyond it had made up his own, had cut out pictures from magazines and written the words beside them in large clear letters. By the time the boy went to school he had known more than any of the rest, he was 'very forward' they had said, though looking him up and down at the same time, he was so small for his age.

It troubled him that the boy was so small; he watched the others as they came out of school and they were all taller, thicker in body and stronger of limb. His face was pale and curiously old-looking beside theirs. He had always looked old.

The old man concerned himself even more with fresh eggs and milk and cheese, fruit and potatoes and watched over the boy while he ate. But he did eat.

'We had meat and cabbage for dinner.'

'Did you finish it up?'

'I had a second helping and then we had cake for pudding. Cake and custard. I don't like that.'

'You didn't leave it on the plate?'

'No. Well, a bit. I just don't like it that's all.'

Now, as they came onto the marshes, the water and sky were even paler and the reeds beside the stream were bleached, like old wood left out for years in the sun. The wind was stronger, whipping at their legs from behind.

'There's the swan.'

'They've a nest somewhere about.'

'Have you seen it?'

'They don't let you see it. They go away from it if anybody walks by.'

'I drew a picture of a swan.'

'Today?'

'No. Once. It wasn't very good.'

'If a thing's not good you should do it again.'

'Why should I?'

'You'll get better then.'

'I won't get better at drawing.' He spoke very deliberately, as he often did, knowing himself and clear about the truth of things, so that the old man was silent, respecting it.

'He's sharp,' Maldrun's wife said. 'He's clever, that one.'

But the old man would not have him too lightly praised. 'He's only a child yet. He's everything to learn.'

'He'll do though, won't he? He's sharp.'

But perhaps it was only the words he used, only the serious expression on his face, which came of so much reading and all that time spent with the old man. And if he was, as they said, so sharp, so forward, perhaps it would do him no good.

He worried about that, wanting the boy to find his

place easily in the world, he tried hard not to shield him from things, made him go to the farm to see Maldrun and over Harper's fen by himself to play with the gamekeeper's boys, told him always to mix with the others at school, to do what they did. Because he was most afraid, at times, of their very contentment together, of the self-contained life they led, for in truth they needed no one, each of them would be entirely happy never to go far beyond this house; they spoke, or were silent, the boy read and made lists, lists of the names of birds or insects, and built elaborate structures, houses and castles, palaces and forts, out of old matchboxes and bits of driftwood. He helped with the garden, had his own corner down beside the shed in which he grew what he chose. It had been like this from the beginning, from the day the old man had brought him here at eight months old and set him down on the floor and helped him to crawl, and then to stand, to walk, they had fallen naturally into their life together. Nobody else had wanted him. Nobody else would have taken such care.

Once people had been suspicious, they had spoken to each other, disapproved.

'He needs a woman there. It's not right. He needs someone who knows about little ones.' Maldrun's wife had said. But now even she had accepted that it was not so and before strangers she would have defended them more fiercely than anyone.

'He's a fine boy that, he's all right. You look at him.

Look. You can't tell what'll work out for the best. You
can never tell.'

By the time they came across the track which led
between the gorse bushes and down through the fir
trees it was as cold as it had been on any night in
January; they brought in more wood for the fire and
had toast and the last of damson jam and mugs of tea.

'It's like winter only not so dark. I like it in winter.'

But it was April now; in the marshes the herons and
redshanks were nesting and the larks spiralled up
singing through the silence. It was almost spring.

So they went on until they had always done until
the fourth of April. Then, on the day after their long
walk out to Derenow, the day after they saw the kingfisher, it happened.

From the early morning he had felt uneasy though
there was no reason he could give for his fear, it simply
lay there, hard and cold as a stone in his belly and he
was restless about the house.

The weather had changed. It was warm, with low,
dun-coloured clouds and a thin mist over the marshes.
He felt the need to get out, to walk and walk; the cottage was oddly quiet. When he went down between the
fruit trees to the bottom of the garden the first of the
buds were breaking into green but the grass was soaked
with dew like sweat, the heavy air smelled rotten and
sweet.

*

They set off in the early morning. The boy did not question, he was always happy to go anywhere at all, but when he was asked to choose their route he set off at once, a few paces ahead, on the path that forked away east in the opposite direction from the village and leading over three miles of empty marsh to the sea. They followed the river bank and the water was sluggish with fronds of dark green weed lying below the surface. The boy bent and put his hand cautiously down, breaking the skin of the water but when his fingers came up against the soft edges of the plants he pulled back.

'Slimy.'

'Yes. It's out of the current here. There's no freshness.'

'Will there be fish?'

'Maybe.'

'I don't like it.' Though for some minutes he continued to peer down between the reeds at the pebbles just visible on the bed of the stream. 'He asks questions,' they said, 'takes an interest in everything. It's his mind, isn't it, bright, you can see. He wants to know.' Though were plenty of times when he said nothing at all, his small, old-young face was crumpled in thought.

'You could die here. You could drown in the water and never never be found.'

'That's not a thing to think about. What do you worry about that for?'

'But you could.'

They were walking in single file, the boy still in front. From all the secret nests down in the reed beds the birds made their own noises, chirring and whispering or sending out sudden cries of warning and alarm. The high, sad call of a curlew came again and again and then ceased abruptly. The boy whistled in imitation.

'Will it answer?'

He whistled again. They waited. Nothing. His face was shadowed with disappointment.

'You can't fool them.'

'You can make a blackbird answer you. You can easily.'

'Not the same.'

'Why isn't it?'

'Blackbirds are garden birds, tamer.'

'Wouldn't a curlew come into the garden?'

'No.'

'Why wouldn't it?'

'Likes to be away from things. They keep to their own places.'

As they went on the air around them seemed to close in further, it seemed harder to breathe and they could not see clearly ahead to where the marshes and mist merged into the sky. Here and there the stream led off into small muddy pools and hollows and the water in them was reddened by the rust seeping from some old can or metal crate thrown there and left for years, the stains which spread out looked like old blood. Gnats jazzed in clusters over the water.

'Will we go onto the beach?'

'We could.'

'We might find something on the beach.'

Often they searched among the pebbles for pieces of amber or jet, for old buckles and buttons and sea-smooth coins washed up by the tides; the boy had a collection of them in a cardboard box in his room.

They walked on and then, out of the thick silence which was all around them came the creaking of wings nearer and nearer and sounding like two thin boards of wood beaten slowly together. A swan, huge as an eagle, came over their heads, flying low, so that the boy looked up for a second in terror at the size and close-ness of it.

He said urgently, 'Swans go for people, swans can break your arm if they beat you with their wings can't they?'

'They don't take any notice of you if you leave them be.'

'But they can can't they?'

'They wouldn't want to.'

He watched the great white shape fly awkwardly away in the direction of the sea.

A hundred yards further on, at the junction of two paths across the marsh there was the ruin of a water-mill, blackened after a fire years before. Inside, under an arched doorway, it was dark and damp, the broken walls were covered with yellowish moss and water lay brackish in the mud hollows of the floor.

At high summer, on hot shimmering days they had come across here on the way to the beach with a string bag of food for their lunch and then the water-mill had seemed like a sanctuary, cool and silent, the boy had stood inside and called softly and listened to the echo of his own voice as it rang lightly round and round the walls.

Now, he stopped dead on the path some distance away.

'I don't want to go.'

'We're walking to the beach.'

'No, I don't want to go past that.'

'The mill?'

'There are rats.'

'Get on.'

'And flying things. Bats.'

'What's to be afraid of in bats? You've seen them in Maldrun's barn often enough. They don't hurt, bats.'

'I want to go back.'

'You don't have to go into the old mill. Who said you did? We'll go on to the sea.'

'I want to go back now.'

He was not often frightened but standing there in the middle of the still, hushed stretch of fenland the old man felt disturbed in himself again by the fear that something would happen, here, where nothing moved and the birds lay hidden, only crying out their weird cries, where things lay under the unmoving water and the press of the air made him sweat down his back. Something would happen to him, something...

What could happen?

Then, not far ahead, they both saw him at the same moment, a man with a gun under his arm, tall and menacing as a crow against the horizon, and as they saw him they also saw two mallards rise in sudden panic from their nest in the reeds and they heard the shots, three shots that cracked out and echoed for miles around, the air went on reverberating with the waves of terrible sound.

The ducks fell, hit in mid-flight. They swerved, turned over and plummeted down. The man with the shotgun started forwards and the grasses and reeds bent and stirred as his dog burrowed to retrieve.

'*I want to go back.*'

Without a word the old man took his hand and they turned and started to walk quickly back the way they had come, as though afraid that they too would be followed and struck down, not caring that they were out of breath and sticky with sweat, only wanting to get away, to reach the shelter of the lane and the trees, to make for home.

Nothing was ever said about it or about the feeling they had both had walking across the marshes. The boy did not mention the man with the gun or the ducks which had been alive and in flight, then so abruptly dead. That evening the old man watched him as he stuck pictures in a book and tore up dock leaves to feed the rabbit, watched for the signs of left-over fear. Perhaps he was quieter than usual, his face closed, more concerned than ever with his own thoughts. In the night he woke, got up and went to the boy and looked down at him through the darkness, for fear that he might have had bad dreams and woken, but there was only the sound of his own breathing; he lay quite still, very straight in the bed.

He imagined the future and his mind filled up with images of all the possible horrors to come, the things which could cause the boy shock and pain and misery and grief and from which he would not be able to protect him, as he had been powerless today to spare him the sight of the two ducks being killed. He was in despair.

Only the next morning he was eased, as it came back to him again, the knowledge that he had, after all, lived out the winter and ahead of them lay light and warmth and greenness.

Nevertheless he half expected that something would happen to them to break into their peace.

For more than a week, nothing did. His fears were quieted. And then the spring broke, the cherry and plum and apple blossom in turn weighed down the branches in great creamy clots, the grass in the orchard sprang up as high as the boy's knees after a couple of nights of soft spring rain and across the marshes and sun shone, the water shone and in the streams it was as clear as glass, the wind blew warmer and smelled of salt and earth. Walking to and from school every day they saw more larks than they had ever seen, quivering in the sky high, high above their heads. Near the gorse bushes, the boy found a nest of leverets. The swallows returned and then the swifts to nest in the slates of the cottage roof and along the lanes, dandelions and but-tercups were golden in the grass.

It was on the Friday that Maldrun gave the boy one of the farm kittens and he carried it home close to his body beneath his coat. It was black and white like Maldrun's cows. And it was the day after that, the end of the first real week of spring, that Blaydon came, Gilbert Blaydon, the boy's father.

He was sitting outside the door watching a buzzard hover above the fir copse when he heard the footsteps. He thought it was Maldrun bringing over the eggs or a chicken – Maldrun generally came over one evening in the week after the boy had gone to bed. They drank a glass of beer and talked for an hour. He was a easy man, undemonstrative. They still called one another formally, 'Mr Maldrun', 'Mr Bowry.'

The buzzard soared backwards and forwards over its chosen patch of air, searching.

When the old man looked down again Blaydon was there, standing in the path. He was carrying a canvas bag.

He knew then why he had been feeling uneasy; he had expected this, or something like it to happen though he had put the fears to the back of his mind with the coming of the sun and the leaf-breaking. He felt no hostility as he looked at the man, only a sudden, desperate weariness.

If anyone had asked he would have said that he would surely never see the boy's father again but now that he was here it did not seem surprising, it seemed, indeed, somehow inevitable. Happiness did not go on.

'Will you be stopping?'

Blaydon walked slowly forwards, hesitated and then set the bag down. He looked much older.

'I don't know if it'd be convenient.'

'There's a room. There's always a room.'

The old man's head buzzed in confusion, he thought he should first offer a drink, or food, or a chair, should see to the room, should ask questions to which he did not want to know the answers. Should say something about the boy.

The boy.

' You've come to take him.'

Blaydon sat down at the other chair beside the out-doors table. The boy looked like him. There was the same narrowness of forehead and chin. Only the mouth was different, though that might be because the boy's was still small and soft, unformed.

'You've come to take him.'

'Where to?' He looked a long time at the old man. 'Where would I have to take him to?'

Only we don't want you here, the old man thought, we don't want anyone, need anyone, and he felt the intrusion of the younger man with the broad hands, and long legs sprawled under the small table, like a violent upheaval in the careful quiet pattern of their lives. He was alien. *We don't want you.*

But what right had he to say that? He did not say it. He was standing up helplessly not knowing what should come next; he felt the bewilderment as some kind of buzzing irritation inside his head.

He felt old.

In the end he said, 'Will you have eaten?'

Blaydon stared at him. 'Don't you want to know where I've come from?'

'No.'

'No.'

'I've made a stew. You'll be better off for a plate of food.'

'Where is he?'

'Asleep in bed, where else would he be at this time? I look after him. I know what I'm about. It's half past eight gone, what else would he be doing at half past eight, he's a child.'

He heard his own voice rising and quickening as he defended himself, defended both of them in a way; he could prove it to this father or to anyone else how he had looked after the boy. He would have asked, what about you, where have you been, whatever did you do for him? But he was too afraid. He guessed what rights Blaydon might have over the boy even though he had never been near, never bothered.

'You could have been dead.'

'Did you think that?'

'I never thought. I knew nothing. Heard less.'

'No.'

Out of the corner of his eye the old man saw the kestrel swoop down into the copse.

The sky was mulberry coloured.

'I wasn't dead.'

The old man saw now that Blaydon looked both tired and dirty. His nails were broken, he was unshaved, the wool at the neck of his sweater was unravelling and there were holes in his jacket sleeves. What was he to say to the boy, then, when he had brought him up to be so tidy and careful and clean, took his clothes to be mended by a woman in the village and had always washed and cut his hair himself? What was he to tell him about this man?

'There's hot water. I'll get you linen, make your bed. You'd better go and wash before I put out the food.'

He went into the kitchen and poured a glass of beer from the jug and was calmed a little by the need to organize things, by the simple, physical activity.

When he took the beer out Blaydon was still

leaning back on the old chair. There were dark stains below his eyes.

'You'd best take it up with you.' The old man held out the beer.

It was almost dark. After a long pause, Blaydon reached out, took the glass and drank, emptying it in four or five long swallows. Then, as though all his muscles were stiff, rose slowly, took up the canvas bag and went into the house.

When the old man had set the table and dished out the food he was trembling. He tried to turn his mind away from the one thought, that Blaydon had come to take the boy away.

He called. When there was no reply he went up the stairs. Blaydon was stretched out on his belly on top of the bed, heavy and motionless in sleep.

The old man worried about the morning. It was Saturday. There would not be the diversion of the walk to school. The boy would wake and come downstairs and confront Blaydon.

What he had originally told him was, your mother died, your father had to go away, and that was the truth. But he doubted if the boy so much as remembered, he had asked a question about it all only once, years ago.

They were content together, needing no one.

He sat on the straight-backed chair in the darkness surrounded by hidden greenery and the scent of honeysuckle and tried to think what he might say.

'This is your father. This is your father who came back. Other boys have fathers. This is your father who will stay with us here.'

The boy would ask for how long.

'Some time. A few days. I don't know.'

He would ask his name.

'Blaydon.'

He would ask what he should call him.

'Blaydon. Mr Blaydon.'

'You should call him …' But his mind broke down before the sheer cliff confronting it and he simply sat on, hands useless in front of him on the table, he thought of nothing and on white plates in the kitchen the stew cooled and congealed and the new kitten from Maldrun's farm slept, curled on an old green jumper. The kitten, the boy, the boy's father, slept. From the copse came the shriek of a fox.

'You didn't eat the meal last night.'

'I slept.'

'You'll be hungry.' He had his back to Blaydon, busy with the frying pan and plates over the stove and with the thought of asking what had made him tired enough to sleep like that from early evening until now, fully clothed on top of the bed. But he would rather not know, would not ask questions.

The back door was open to the path that led down between vegetable beds and bean canes and currant bushes towards the thicket. Blaydon went to stand there.

'Two eggs will you have?'

'If…'

'There's plenty.' He wanted to divert him, talk to him, he had to pave the way. The boy was out there, somewhere at the end of the garden.

'We'd a hard winter.'

'Yes?'

'Knee deep, January, February, we'd to dig ourselves out of that door. And then it froze. The fens froze right over, ice as thick as your fist. I've never known like it.'

But now it was spring, now, outside, there was the glorious green of new grass, new leaves, now the sun shone.

He began to set out knives and forks on the kitchen table. It would have to come. He would have to call the boy in, to bring them together. What would he say? His heart seemed to squeeze, then pump hard suddenly in the thin bone-cage of his chest.

Blaydon's clothes were creased and crumpled. They were not clean. Had he washed himself?

'I thought I'd get a job,' Blaydon said.

The old man watched him.

'Look for work.'

'Here?'

'Around here. Is there work?'

'Maybe. I've had no reason to look. Maybe.'

'If I'm staying on I'll need to work.'

'Yes.'

'It'd be a help, I daresay.'

'You've a right to do as you think fit. Make up your own mind.'

'Pay my way.'

'You've no need to worry about the boy. He's all right, he's provided for. You've no need to find money for him.'

'All the same.'

Blaydon walked over and sat down at the table.

The old man thought, he is young and fit, strong, he's come here to stay and he has every right. He is the boy's father. He is…

He did not want Blaydon in their lives, did not want the man's hands resting on the table and the big feet on the floor beneath it.

He said, 'You could try at the farm. Maldrun's farm. They've maybe got work. You could ask.'

'Maldrun's.'

'It'd be ordinary work. Labouring work.'

'I'm not choosy.'

The old man put fried eggs and bread onto the plates, poured tea, filled the basin with sugar. And then he had no more to do, he had to call in the boy.

But nothing happened as he had feared.

He came in.

'Wash your hands now.' But he was already half way to the sink, he had been brought up so carefully, the order was not an order but a formula between them, regular, a comfort. 'Wash your hands now.'

'Hello.'

The boy stopped turning his hands round the soap.

'I came last night. Got here. I've come to stay for a bit.'

The boy went on washing his hands, rinsing, drying them on the towel above the stove. After that he turned round and looked from one to the other of them, trying to assess this sudden change in the order of things.

'Eat your food,' the old man said.

'How long have you come for?'

'A bit.'

'What's your name?'

'Gilbert Blaydon.'

'What have I to call you?'

'Either.'

'Gilbert Blaydon.'

'What you like.'

They got on with eating then.

Maldrun took him on at the farm and then their lives formed a new pattern. Blaydon got up before them and was gone before the boy was down, before he and the old man ate and then set off across the marsh to school. They were alone together, that was as it had always been. Blaydon did not return until late.

When he was not working he went off somewhere alone. At the weekend, he sometimes took the boy for walks. They saw the herons' nest, the cygnets, a peregrine flying over the estuary. The two of them were at ease together.

Alone, the old man tried to imagine what they might be saying to each other, he walked distractedly about the house, almost weeping with anxiety and dread. They came down the path and the boy was sitting on Blaydon's shoulders laughing and laughing.

'You've told him.'

Blaydon turned, surprised and shooed the boy away. 'I've said nothing.'

The old man believed him. But there was still a fear for the future, the end of things.

The days lengthened. The school holidays went by, during which the old man was happiest because he had so much time alone with the boy. In the mornings, there was sometimes a fine mist over the marsh.

'He's a good worker' Maldrun said, coming over one evening with the eggs and finding the old man alone, 'I'm glad to have him.'

'Yes.'

'Takes a bit off your shoulders.'

'He pays his way.'

'I meant work. Work and worries. All of that.'

What did Maldrun know? But he only looked back at the old man, his face open and friendly, drinking his beer.

He realised that it was true. He had grown used to having Blaydon about to carry the heavy things and lock up at night, to clear the fruit loft and lop off over-hanging branches and cut back the brambles at the entrance to the thicket.

He had slipped through a crack into their lives and established himself there. Now, when he thought of the future without Blaydon it was to worry for the summer was always short and then came the run down through autumn into winter again. Into snow and ice and cold and the north-east wind scything across from the marshes. He dreaded it now that he was old. Last winter he had been ill once and for only a short time. This winter he was a year older and anything might happen. He thought of the mornings when he would have to take the boy to school before it was even light, thought of the frailty of his own flesh, the brittleness of his bones; he looked in the mirror and his own weak and rheumy eyes looked back.

He began to count on Blaydon's being here to ease things, to help with the coal and wood and the break-ing of ice on pails of water, to be in some way an insur-ance against his own possible illness, possible death.

Though now it was only early summer, now he watched Blaydon build a rabbit hutch for the boy, hammering nails and sawing wood, uncoiling wire skilfully. He heard them laugh together. This was what he needed after all, not a woman about the place but a man, the strength and ease of a man who was not old, did not fear, did not say, 'Drink up your milk,' 'Eat up your food,' 'Be careful.'

The kitten grew and spun round in quick, mad circles in the sun.

'He's a good worker,' Maldrun said.

After a while the old man took to dozing n his chair outside after supper while Blaydon washed up and tidied, then took out the shears to clip the hedge or the grass borders, dig potatoes.

But everything that had to do with the boy, the business of rising and eating, going to school and returning, the routine of clothes and food and drink and bed, all that was still supervised by the old man. Blaydon did not interfere, scarcely seemed to notice what was done. His own part in the boy's life was quite different.

In July, it was hotter than the old man could ever remember. The gnats swarmed in soft grey clouds under the trees and over the still water on the marshes. The sun shone hard and bright from dawn and the light played tricks so that the estuary seemed now very near, now far away. Maldrun's cows tossed their heads against the flies which gathered stickily in runnels below their great eyes.

He began to rely more and more upon Blaydon as the summer reached its height, left more jobs for him to do, because he was willing and strong and because the old man succumbed easily now to rest in the hot sun. He still did most of the cooking but he would let

Blaydon go down to the shops and the boy often went with him. He was growing, his limbs were filling out and his skin was berry-brown. He lost the last softness of babyhood. He had accepted Blaydon's presence without question and was entirely used to him, though he did not show any less affection for the old man, who continued to take care of him day by day, but he became less hesitant, more self-assured, he spoke of things in a casual, confident voice, learned much from his talks with Blaydon. He still did not know that this was his father. The old man saw no reason to tell him – not yet, not yet; they could go on as they were for the time being, just as they were.

He was comforted by the warmth of the sun on his face, by the scent of the roses and of the tobacco plants in the evening, the sight of the scarlet bean-flowers clambering higher and higher up their frame.

He had decided from the beginning that he himself would ask no questions of Blaydon, would wait until he was told.

But he was not told. Blaydon's life might have only begun on the day he had arrived here. The old man wondered if he had been abroad, working on a ship, or even in prison though there was no evidence for any of it. In the evenings they drank beer together and some-times played a game of cards, though more often Blaydon worked in the garden and the old man simply sat watching him, hearing the last cries of the birds from the marshes.

With the money Blaydon brought in they bought new clothes for the boy and better cuts of meat and then one afternoon a television set arrived, with two men in a green van, to erect an aerial.

'For the winter,' Blaydon said, 'maybe you won't bother now but it'll be company for the winter.'

'I've never felt the lack.'

'All the same.'

'I don't need company, don't need entertainment, when we wanted it we made our own, always made our own.'

'You'll be glad of it, once you've got the taste.'

The old man started to look at it sometimes, late at night, and discovered some things of interest to him, new horizons were opened, new worlds.

'I'd not have known that,' he would say, 'or that. I've never travelled. Look at the things I'd never have known.'

Blaydon nodded. He himself seemed uninterested in the television. He was mending the front fence, staking it the whole way along with wood Maldrun had given him from the farm. Now the gate would fit close and not swing and bang in the gales of the coming winter.

It was one night towards the end of August when Blaydon mentioned the trip to the seaside.

'He's never been,' he said, wiping the foam of beer off his top lip. 'I asked him. He's never seen the sea.'

'I've done all I could. There's not been the money.'

'I'm not blaming you.'

'I'd have taken him, I've have seen to it in time. Sooner or later.'

'Yes.'

'Yes.'

'Well, I could take him.'

'To the sea?'

'Yes.'

'For a day? It's far enough.'

'A couple of days. A weekend.'

The old man was silent. It was true, the boy had never been anywhere and perhaps he suffered as a result, perhaps the others at school talked of where they had gone and what they had seen, shaming him. If that was so then he should be taken, should go everywhere, he must not miss anything, not be left out.

'We'd leave first thing Saturday come back Monday. I'd take the days off.'

'You do as you think best.'

'I'd do nothing without asking you.'

'It's only right. He's at the age for taking things in. He needs enjoyment.'

'Yes.'

'You go. It's right.'

'I haven't told him.'

'Then tell him.'

When he did the boy's face opened with pleasure, he

licked his lips nervously over and over again in his excitement, already counting the time until they were to go. The old man sorted out clothes for him, washed them and hung them out, began himself to anticipate. This was right. The boy ought to go.

But he dreaded it. They had never been separated before. He could not imagine how it would be now, to sleep alone in the cottage, and then he began to imagine all the possible accidents that might come about.

Blaydon had not asked him if he wanted to go with them. But he did not. He felt suddenly too tired to leave the cottage, too tired for journeys or strangers. He wanted to sit on his chair in the sun and mark the time until they should be back.

He had got used to the idea of Blaydon's continuing presence here, he no longer lived in dread of the coming winter. It seemed a lifetime since he had been alone here with the boy.

They set off very early on the Saturday morning before the sun had broken through the thick mist over the marshes. Every sound was clear and separate as it came through the air, he heard their footsteps, the brush of their legs against the grasses long after they were out of sight. The boy had his own bag bought new in the village, a canvas bag strapped across his shoulders. He stood up very straight, eyes shining, his mind filled with imaginary pictures of what he would see, what they would do.

*

The old man went back into the kitchen and put the kettle on again, refilled the teapot for himself and planned his day. He would work; he would clean out all the bedrooms and sort the boy's clothes, setting aside any he had grown out of, any that needed mending; he would polish the cutlery and take down and wash the curtains and walk to the village for groceries, he would bake bread, a cake and pies, prepare a stew, ready for their return.

So that, on the first day, the Saturday, he scarcely had space in his mind to think of them, to notice their absence, and in the evening his legs and back ached, he sat only for a short time outside after his meal, drunk with tiredness and slept later than usual on Sunday morning.

It was only then that he began to feel the silence and emptiness of the house. He walked about it uselessly, he woke up the kitten and teased it with a feather so that it would play with him, distract his attention from his own solitude. When it slept again he went out and walked for miles across the still, hot marshes. The water between the reed beds was very low and even dried up altogether in places, revealing the dark greenish-brown slime below. The faint, dry whistling sound that usually came through the rushes was absent. He felt as parched as the countryside after the long, long summer. The sweat ran down his bent back.

He had walked in order to tire himself out again

but this night he slept badly and woke out of clinging nightmares with a thudding heart, tossed from side to side, uncomfortable among the sheets. But tomorrow he could begin to count the strokes of the clock until their return.

He got up feeling as if he had never slept; his eyes were blurred and pouchy beneath. But he began the baking, the careful preparations for their return home. He scarcely stopped for food himself all day, though his head and back still ached, he moved stiffly about the kitchen.

When they had not returned by midnight on the Monday he did not go down to the village or across to Maldrun's farm to telephone the police. He did nothing. He knew.

But he sat up in the chair outside the back door all night, with the silence pressing in on his ears. Once or twice his head nodded down onto his chest and he almost slept, but then jerked awake again, shifted a little and sat on in the darkness.

They had not taken everything; clothes were left, clothes, toys, books, they must mean to come back. But he knew that they did not. Other toys, other clothes, could be bought anywhere.

A week passed and the summer slid imperceptibly into autumn like smooth cards shuffled together in a pack, the trees faded to yellow, dried and curled at the edges. Fell.

He did not leave the house and he ate almost nothing, only filled and refilled the teapot. In the evenings he drank tea, not beer.

He did not blame Gilbert Blaydon, he blamed himself for having thought to keep the boy, for having planned their whole future. When the father had turned up he should have known at once what he wanted, should have said, 'Take him away, take him now,' to save them from this furtiveness, this deception. In the nights though, he wondered what effect it would have on the boy who had been brought up so scrupulously, to be tidy and clean, to eat up his food, to learn. To tell the truth. He wished there was an address to which he could write a list of details about the boy's everyday life, the routine he was used to following.

He waited for a letter. None came. The trees sagged under their weight of ripe, dark fruit and after a time the plums and apples and pears fell with soft thuds onto the grass. He did not gather it up as usual and take the apples to store in the loft, he left it for the sweet pulp to be burrowed by hornets and grubs. But sometimes he took a pear and ate it, standing beneath the tree, for he had never approved of waste.

He kept the boy's room exactly as it should be. His clothes were clean and laid out neatly in the drawers, his books and toys lined on the shelves in case he returned. But he did not bother with the rest of the house. Dirt began to linger in corners, fluff grey beneath beds. The damp on the bathroom wall was grown over with moss like a fungus when the first week of rain came.

Maldrun had been across two or three times from the farm but received no reply to his questions. In the village the women talked. October went out in drizzle and fog and the next time Maldrun came the old man did not open the door. Maldrun waited, peering through the windows of the cottage between cupped hands and in the end left the eggs on the back step.

The old man got up later each day and went to bed earlier, to sleep between frowsty, unwashed sheets. For a while he turned on the television set in the evenings and sat staring at whatever was offered to him but in the end did not bother, only sat on in the kitchen with the dark around him. Outside, the last of the fruit fell onto the sodden grass and lay there untouched, rotting.

Winter came.

In the small town flat, Blaydon set out plates, cut bread and opened tins, filled the pan with milk.

'Wash your hands,' he said.

But the boy was already there, at the basin, moving his palms over the over the pink soap, obediently, wondering what was for tea.

HALLORAN'S CHILD

He was eating the rabbit he had shot himself on the previous day, separating the small bones carefully from the flesh before soaking lumps of bread in the dark salt gravy. When they were boys, he and his brother, Nelson Twomey, used to trap rabbits and other animals too, weasels and stoats – it was sport, they thought nothing of it, it was only what Farley the gamekeeper did.

Then, Nate had gone by himself into the wood and found a young fallow deer caught by the leg, and when he had eventually got it free the animal had stumbled away, its foot mangled and dropping a trail of blood through the undergrowth. Nate had gone for his brother, brought him back there and shown him.

'Well, it'll die, that's what,' Nelson had said, and shrugged his thin shoulders. It was the first glimpse Nate had had of his brother's true nature, his meanness.

'Die of gangrene. That's poison.'

He had wept that night, one of the few occasions in his life, and got up at dawn and gone out to search for the wounded animal, remembering the trembling hind quarters and the sweat which had matted its pale coat, the eyes, where sticky rheum had begun to gather in the corners. He found only the blood, dried dark on the bracken. It led him towards where the bank of the stream fell away at his feet, and he could not follow further.

After that he abandoned the traps, though there was nothing he could do to stop his brother from setting them, even if he had been able to talk to him. He was very tall, with long, pale hairless arms and legs, and beaky features, and he spoke little. He kept his violence well hidden. When he left school he went as apprentice to Layce, the rat-catcher, and took over the job himself three years afterwards when Layce died. Then, for forty-eight years, he had left the village at seven each morning, the rat bag over his shoulder, and the two small dogs at his heels. He always wore the same long, beige raincoat and cap, and when one of the ratting dogs died, it was replaced by another identical dog, so that to everyone in the village the two seemed to have lived forever. He had always given his dogs the same names – Griff and Nip.

Over the years, Nelson Twomey began to stoop at the shoulders until a few years before his death he was bent almost double. His face was sallow and expressionless.

Once, Nate had gone with him to watch the rat-catching in a grain barn over at Salt, and been half-excited, half-sickened at the sight of the dogs, inching forwards, bellies to the ground, snuffling, waiting for the command, and then darting forward like arrows, teeth bared, down onto the hidden rats. He could still remember the look on his brother's face as he stood half in the shadows, thin and pale and grave as a ghost, unmoving; he could still smell the musty smell of the grain. He sensed that Nelson enjoyed it, that his job satisfied some appalling need with him. But he was highly thought of, because of his skills, and well-paid too, for rats were a menace and greatly feared. Nate himself went in terror of them until he was a grown man. But he never ceased to be afraid, also, of his brother, so that it was almost a relief when he died and the cottage was empty of him.

But Nate Twomey continued to shoot rabbits, that he did not mind, for he had a keen eye and a sure hand, the animals never lingered, half-alive, and besides, they were pests, there had to be some way of putting them down. Nor did he mind wringing the necks of the hens his sister kept. It was only the traps that he regretted, the traps reminded him that he had been linked by blood to his brother.

The flesh of the rabbit fell away moistly from the bones. But in the middle of eating he had to raise his handkerchief to his left eye again and again, where the chip of wood had flown into it that morning, leaving it watery and sore. So that when Bertha spoke to him, he could not see her face and so missed what she was saying. He read her lips more easily than those of anyone else, she had only to mumble and he knew, for it was she who had first taught him, and shown him how to write, too, she had been more patient with his deafness and dumbness than either of their parents, who were uneasy, never knowing what he might be thinking, and frightened of being judged and blamed by the rest of the village. There had been one other child, also a boy, who had died, but he had been quite sound, they felt bitter that it was Nate who grew up in place of him.

Bertha Twomey waited. She always ate her own meal alone, after her brother had gone back to the workshop, and now, she stood beside the wooden kitchen table until he had finished wiping his eyes.

'You damaged yourself then, haven't you?'

He pointed to his eye.

'Splinters. You want to be more careful – putting your head too close to that bench, that's what. I told you before about that.'

He shook his head but his eye was watering freely, he had to wipe it again, and then she insisted on looking at it more closely. It was bloodshot and swimming with tears. In the end, she got the splinter out with the twisted corner of a clean handkerchief. 'You be more careful what you're doing in future, Nate Twomey.' He grinned, nodding at her. They had always been like this together, she treating him like a child, while still knowing that he was not a fool, just because he was deaf and dumb. She was two years older but she had been the first one to push him out, not so long after she had learned to walk herself, they were very close.

Bertha Twomey always wore black – long, full skirts and loose cardigans and heavy black shoes on her wide, painful feet, and so she had looked like an old woman for years. There were lines in her face, they had come there when she was still a young girl, but she had been pretty and her face still had distinction, though she wore her hair scraped back and knotted behind her head, making herself severe.

When she was nineteen, she had been married to Hale, the farrier's son, from Salt, there had been a supper on trestle tables set out in Mid New Common one hot June night, and dancing until sunset, and then Nate had gone to live with them, for his sister had said she would never leave him. Hale had not objected. Nate had an attic room and helped out with the horses, before being apprenticed to Rob Riddy, who was undertaker for all the villages around. Bertha's husband had taught Nate how to shoot. And then, only a year later, he was dead, killed by lightning up on the Top Field, and the very next day, Nate and Bertha had moved back to their own family.

He looked up at her now, at the wide, serious face with the lined forehead, the strong bones. He had never known what she felt about her husband's death, never seen her weeping and she had told him nothing.

She had taken a domestic post at the Lodge, and done most of the housework for her mother too, as though she could not bear to be idle for a moment. Otherwise, she had kept herself to herself and looked after Nate. But she had changed, age had come to her overnight, and she had never gone out of black.

His eye was easier, it no longer watered. He took up a spoonful of gooseberries, thick with syrup.

Bertha said, 'The doctor was sent for to Halloran's.'

He stopped eating. So she had been waiting to tell him this then.

'I haven't heard more.'

The fruit had turned sickly in his mouth, he could not swallow it. His sister sat down and watched him. She knew. Nate shook his head.

'You'd best finish it.' But she saw that he could not and, after a moment or two, got up slowly and took the dish away.

Nate went to the back door and opened it, and the sun shone full into his face, comforting him, he smelled the fruit bushes and the scarlet bean flowers. At the bottom of the garden the hens were russet coloured, like squirrels, scratching about. He went down to them. When he opened the gate in the wire they took no notice of him at all, only went on pecking at the soil for the last of the meal Bertha had thrown. The sun was very hot here, the air still and dry. Nate's ears rang with silence.

Halloran's child. He tried to believe that it was nothing, that she would certainly be well and coming to talk to him in the workshop, soon enough, that he would see her sitting up on the bench watching his hands move to and fro, planing a piece of oak. But nobody sent for the doctor until it was unavoidable and besides, she had been out of hospital for less than a month.

He stared down at the hens.

In the kitchen, Bertha Twomey cleared the dinner table and took the blue and white checked cloth to shake outside the back door, at the same time looking down the garden at her brother, and then she felt all the old anxiety for him lying heavy as a stone in her chest, though he was sixty-eight years and she was nearly seventy.

There had always been Twomeys here, but neither Nate nor Nelson the rat-catcher had married, and so they would be the last. She had not wanted to tell him about the Halloran child but he would take it better from her than from some stranger coming into the workshop, and, in any case, there was no hope, it was certain that the child would die, though no one knew when.

The thing she was most afraid of was that he would want to go to the Halloran house. He could not do so, because they were Twomeys, because of the way people thought of him and the work he did, because of all the old suspicion.

He was still standing motionless in the hen run, his head bent under the hot sun. She thought, say something to him, tell him…But she would not. He knew for himself. He was deaf and dumb but a grown man. The midday air stirred a little, moving the long lines of tinfoil tops, set across the vegetable patches to scare the birds away. Say something to him.

But she turned and went back inside.

*

It was common knowledge that a Twomey had been taken for a witch and some said burned, some said drowned to death. So there were superstitions about the family which died hard and when Bertha Twomey's husband was struck by lightning, what people felt was somehow confirmed and they kept their distance. Now, to the children in the village, Bertha looked like a witch, they stared at her from a safe distance, awed by the black clothes, and had nightmares too, in which she set evil upon them. All of it she knew and was accustomed to it, it only served to make her draw further inside herself. She spoke to no one, not even to her brothers, about how she was feeling. And to them both she had been a rock, taking the place of mother and father and wife, they could not imagine her capable of any weakness.

From Nate Twomey, too, people kept their distance but that was because of the work he did, for he himself was amiable enough, and harmless, nobody blamed him because he could not hear or speak. Nevertheless, the odd noises which he made, the grunts and choking sounds in his throat, which were how he tried to imitate what he saw of laughter, frightened the children. All except Halloran's child.

The Hallorans had come down in the world. Their grandfather had owned land, kept a few dairy cows and called himself a farmer. But when his son inherited, there were more debts than profits, and the land had to be sold. Arthur Halloran had lost his heart very quickly, watching his father struggle, and when he was seventeen he left the village altogether and went for a sailor. He returned with a damaged leg, married Amy Criddick and now he was only a casual labourer, working on hedging or hay-making or picking potatoes and paid by the hour. He was a bad-tempered, disappointed man, suffered in the village rather than liked. They had one child, the daughter, Jenny. She had never been strong, never been truly well since the day she was born, and when she was a year old and began to walk her limbs seemed incapable of holding her up, she was unsteady and sickly. At the age of four she had rheumatic fever and almost died and Halloran had said in public that he wished for it, wished to have it over with, for who wanted an invalid for a child and how could he bear the anxiety? She had been forbidden to run or even walk far, though she went to school when she was five and there was treated like a fragile doll by the others, who had been put in awe of her. She played with no one, though sometimes, as she sat in the class-room or, in fine weather, on a little stool in the corner of the playground, one of them would take pity on her and bring pick-sticks or a jigsaw and do it with her for a little while. But she seemed to be separated from them, almost to be less than human, because of the fine blueness tingeing her lips and the flesh below her nervous eyes. She was neither clever nor stupid, she said very little. In the end, they were bored by her.

Then, she began to visit Nate Twomey in the car-penter's shop at the back of Coker's Lane. He could say nothing to her, which seemed to put her at her ease, for she would talk to him more than to anyone else in her life, fascinated by the way he looked straight at her and watched the movements of her lips. She learned what the grunts meant which he uttered occasionally, whether they expressed his approval or not, though most often he would simply nod or shake his head and smile at her, before he went on with his sawing or plan-ing or the hammering in of nails. If there was ever any question that needed a fuller reply, he stopped and wrote it down carefully on a page of his measurement book, with the thick, flat carpenter's pencil.

In the holidays she came almost every day. He gave her a drink of tea from the flask his sister put up for him, and grew used to her presence, it pleased him, made him feel somehow at ease, settled. She sat on the workbench – he had to lift her up there, and she weighed nothing, she was made of air, he was shocked at the frailness of her body between his huge hands.

For much of the time they were both of them silent. She liked the smell of the workshop and the rasping sound of the plane driving evenly over a plank of wood. Only the high-pitched scream of the electric saw terrified her, she would stuff her fingers into her ears and her head rang, though Nate only looked at her and grinned, bending his own head right down over the blade, hearing nothing. He could only try to imagine how the noise pained her by feeling the saw's vibration jar through his body.

Nate was the coffin-maker. Usually, at least once a week, there was a death in one of the villages, and he went there on his bicycle, removing his cap respectfully when he reached the front door, before going inside to measure up and received the family requirements, written out for him on a slip of paper. The sight of death had never alarmed him, he had been used to it for so long and it quieted him, for he felt that if a man came only to this, this state of calmness and silence, there could be no harm, and nothing in the world could damage him.

And when he leaned over the bodies of the dead, when his hands touched them gently as he worked, he took into himself through them the certainty of resurrection, so that he returned to his workshop to make the coffin confidently, and with a sense of awe. He knew that he was a good craftsman and his work satisfied him when it was finished, it seemed altogether useful, altogether good.

But now, he could not conceive of death in relation to Jenny Halloran, he disbelieved in the possibility of it, though she was so frail. He had always loved her, they had accepted one another completely, and so he could not accept that she might die, or even worse, might suffer in her body. He was reminded again of the trapped deer.

A year ago, the child had been taken ill with some severe, unidentifiable pain and then, three times in the space of a couple of months, she had fallen over and broken bones which were now as brittle as the bones of birds and would not heal, only crumbled slowly apart within their encasing flesh. She was no longer able to walk or even to sit up in a chair unattended, for fear that she would fall out and, in the end, she was pushed about the village in a wheel chair by her mother – for Halloran himself was ashamed, he would have nothing to do with her. And they refused to let her visit the carpenter's workshop again.

Nate Twomey missed her. But if he thought about it while he was working alone, he knew that it was only what he should have expected, that it was surprising, indeed, that they had ever let her come here at all. For he was a Twomey and Twomeys were not trusted, though none of them had done harm to anyone. But a Twomey had been taken for a witch, and Bertha's husband had been struck down and Nate was born deaf and dumb. It was enough to make anyone wary, and glad that the Twomeys' cottage was a little way out of the village.

But Nate knew that what kept them most in dread of him was his job, for many people believed that if they came face to face with the coffin-maker, it meant death to follow and if you let him into your house, other than on his official business, you were surely tempting fate. Halloran was more suspicious than most men, he expected ill-luck because it was what his family had become accustomed to.

The child had come out of hospital, looking even paler and thinner than before, and now people began to keep a little way from her, too, as she was pushed out on fine days in her chair, for she had the look of death about her. Once, Nate met her as he was walking home for dinner and he was shocked at the sight of her, at the small legs poking out like sticks and the neck bent like a stalk, the deadness within the child's eyes. Hers was the only suffering he could not accept. When he went home, he sat pulling at the edges of the tablecloth, rubbing his fingers together, or else standing at the back door, staring down into the garden. He seemed to Bertha to have lost heart for anything.

When she sent him to pick beans or strip the gooseberry and blackcurrant bushes of their fruit, he went heavily down the path and worked mechanically, without any enthusiasm, along the rows. In the old days he would not have to be told, the fruit would be there ready for her, glistening and ripe in great bowls on the kitchen table.

For the first time in his life, too, he began to resent his own condition, to envy those who could hear and chat among themselves, to feel bitter. Why had he been born a Twomey? Why was the child ill and no longer permitted to visit him, what had he done to deserve any of it?

Now, on the day his sister told him the news about the doctor, he was reluctant to go back to his workshop, not wanting to be alone. But old Bart, the stockman from Faze Farm, was dead of a stroke, the funeral was on Wednesday and the coffin was not yet done. Nate envied Bart, who was a year his junior, for it seemed to him suddenly that death was an enviable condition, that Bart was well off and not many had any benefit in this world. He wanted to die himself. He felt exhausted.

While he worked away on the coffin, the idea was growing within him, as his sister had feared it would, that he must go round to the Hallorans' cottage, must see the child, see her now, while she was alive and could still speak to him. He would watch her lips moving and be comforted and besides, he wanted reassurance that she was not in pain, that everything was being done for her. He worked on until his head was full to overflowing with pictures of her and he could not concentrate upon his job, was scarcely aware of the smooth wood beneath his fingers, the coldness of the nails. Bart was six and a half feet tall, it was a big coffin, taking shape upon the bench.

He kept the workshop door open so that a beam of sunlight fell onto the pale curled wood chips that strewed the floor, and warmed his back, too – it was a day he would normally have enjoyed, for the sun always soothed him. But in the end it was too much, in the end he had to go and see Jenny Halloran. At twenty minutes past three, he put his saw away, picked his cap off the hook and blew the dust off it, went out of the door.

The paving stones baked in the heat. There was no one else about as he walked slowly down through the village, a tall, shambling man, his head a little bent, and inside his head, the throbbing of silence.

He went up the front path, put his hand to the door-knocker and then drew it away again. No one saw him. The small front garden was overgrown, with stocks and petunias trying to struggle through thistles and bindweed. Halloran had lost heart.

Because he could not speak, he began to sweat with anxiety that they would not understand why he had come here, would not let him in. He looked up at the bedroom window of the cottage. There were net curtains. Nothing moved. A thin brown cat regarded him from the broken-down fence.

But he could not bear to go away, back to the workshop, without having seen her.

*

It was some minutes after his knocking ceased before Amy Halloran came to the door, opening it only an inch and peering out. When she saw Nate, her face twitched involuntarily and then closed up in fear, or dislike, he could not tell. She was not an old woman, she was not yet forty, but she looked old, her hair was streaked with grey and her rather square face had long, deep lines, from nose to mouth. Nate took off his cap and moved it nervously round and round in his hands.

'Nate Twomey.'

He smiled. He was very hot and the air was dusty as he breathed it in, and thick with the scent of flowers.

'She's in her bed. She's ill. Doctor came.'

He nodded and pointed into the house and then himself. She hesitated still, her expression changing as she thought about it, he could see suspicion and tiredness and worry chasing one another like clouds across her face. People needed to speak, he needed to reassure her, for he was anxious that she should not be afraid of him,

But in the end she let him in, opening the door slowly and then leading him up the dark stairs. The carpet only reached as far as the bend, and then there were bare boards. The house smelled of old cooking and something else, some medicine or disinfectant. He knew that she was uncertain whether she had done right to let him in.

He was appalled at the sight of the child. She lay in an iron-framed bed, propped up on a single pillow, and she seemed to have shrunk, her flesh was thinner, scarcely covering her bones, and the skin was taut and shiny. Her eyes were very bright, and yet dead too, there seemed to be no life in her at all. He looked down at her hand, resting on the sheet. It was like a small claw.

'Here's that friend of yours.'

Nate stood uncertainly, cap still in his hand, he wanted to weep. Her lips moved and there was no blood in them, they were thin and dry and oddly transparent, like the skin of a chrysalis.

'I had the doctor come.'

He nodded to encourage her, for while she could speak to him she was alive, there was hope for her. Amy Halloran stood by the door, only staring vacantly at her child. She seemed too tired, even to worry.

'I'm going to the sea. One day. I'm going on a holiday.'

But it seemed to Nate that she did not believe what she told him, that she knew the truth. She turned her head slightly to look out of the window and for a long time she said nothing else, so that he began to be afraid that she was dead. His hands felt weak and sweaty. The room was very hot.

'Will you make me something? Will you make me a toy?'

For he had occasionally taken bits of surplus wood and carved out a rough doll's cradle or a model bird for her, though they were clumsy, he was not good with such delicate work. But she had always been pleased with them. Now he nodded and tried to shape his hands like a boat, looking at her intently, willing her to understand. She frowned. Then, abruptly, began to cough and her face went into a spasm of pain, the bones seemed to tighten, and her mother went to her and lifted her up, touched her hands again and again to the child's cheeks and forehead. He saw that her eyelids looked dusty and faintly mauve, beneath the skin.

'You've seen enough, Nate Twomey. Haven't you stayed here long enough?'

Nate turned at once and went out of the room, his face burning. But as he reached the foot of the stairs, the front door opened and Halloran stood there, with the bright sunlit garden behind him like the background of a picture.

Nate thought that the man was going to hit him. His face went dark and mottled with blood and he clenched his fist. But then, he knew what Halloran was thinking – that the child was dead, for why else would the coffin-maker be here, standing at the bottom of the stairs that led to her bedroom. He put out his hand, thinking to touch Halloran's shoulder, he pointed back up the staircase and smiled, shaking his head, he would have said, 'I saw her, she was speaking to me. I saw her, she is not dead, she is not dead.'

Halloran started forward. Stopped. Looked up, to see his wife there. The three of them stood, unable to move or speak, helpless. The air shimmered with heat in rings like haloes, over the flowerbeds.

Then, Halloran began to shout, though Nate could only see the anger, see his mouth opening and closing, the corners twisted, so that he could scarcely read what the man was saying.

'Get him out of this house. What did you want to let him in for, what right has he got to come here, what have I told you about him? He's not to see her. He can't be trusted. What are you doing letting a Twomey into this house?'

He swung round. Nate was half-way down the front path. The hollyhocks were full of bees, he watched their circling, though he could not imagine their noise. His heart thudded violently, though not because of Halloran's anger. He felt ashamed of himself, ashamed that he should be able to walk out, healthy and strong, while the child lay dying.

The door of the cottage slammed shut.

He could not go back to work, he was trembling and his head swam with the shock of seeing the child, he began to walk aimlessly out of the village in the direction of Salt, between the thick hawthorn hedges, which trailed convolvulus down on to the grass. The cows were all lying down, flies jazzing about their heavy heads under the trees. His own throat was sore and there was a pain in his chest which seemed to choke him. He knew that he had seen the child for the last time.

That evening he could not eat, he only drank two mugs of sweet tea and left the meat and potatoes and pie his sister had put out for him. What he had begun to feel was some sort of rage boiling up within him, he wanted to get up and beat his fists on something, to lash out in protest at his own dumbness, his own misery.

He rolled up his shirt sleeves and went off to the bottom of the garden and into the hen run, captured one of the birds and held it down in a flurry of feathers and clawing feet. From the kitchen doorway Bertha Twomey watched silently, as he wrung the animal's neck. She knew what had happened and could do nothing for him, she only recognized in him the violence that had also been in his brother. Nate was not the same, he was a gentle man, patient, and so he killed the bird swiftly and without pain. But there had been a rage in him, a viciousness she had never seen before. When he came back into the house carrying the dead bird by its feet, she drew back and told him to put it away in the scullery, she would pluck it the next day when the feathers and flesh were no longer warm.

'You'd best eat something.'

He shook his head and his eyes were clouded with unhappiness. He went out again carrying his gun, and shot crows and jays and pigeons in Faze's fields and over towards the woods, until dark, his aim was as sure as ever, though he had to grip his hands tightly around the gun barrel to quieten their trembling. He was sick with shame at himself, but he went on until he was exhausted, knowing that he had to work out his anger and frustration. When the gun went off, he only saw the puff of smoke and felt his finger jerk sharply back from the trigger. A bird fell somewhere but there was no sound, no sound.

In the west, over High Crop Wood, the sky went dark as damsons, spreading like a stain. The air smelled sweet.

When the gun was empty he went home, his arms and legs aching and his head numb. He was no longer angry. He felt nothing at all. In the kitchen, he tried to eat a slice of pie which his sister had left out for him under a cloth, but his throat contracted, he had to spit the mouthful out. His eyes were still dry and smarting and when he tried to soothe them by weeping, he could not do so, he only lay in his bed, staring up into the darkness remembering the child.

He woke, not abruptly but gradually out of sleep, and when he opened his eyes he saw that the room was filled with still, pale moonlight. Then he knew. He had been awakened by the death of the child. He lay filled with a sense of relief, as though he had recovered from a long fever.

If he put out his hand, he might touch her. If he could speak to her, she would reply. But he could only think, inside his own head, and so she was there too. Above all, he was thankful that she had suffered no longer. That afternoon she had not seemed to be in pain, only weakened, tired.

Often in his life Nate had known about death. When his brother Nelson Twomey died in the hospital at Garston he had been selecting a piece of timber for a door panel in the Rectory, and he had known, his head had been filled with the awareness of his brother, whom he had both hated and loved, respected and feared, and when he had gone to the hospital the next day, they had told him the time of the death and it had been the same.

Now, he got up and went to the window. It was open and the scent of stocks drifted up into his face. The moon rode high over the wood. The night was quiet with the presence of this new death.

He had gone out to shoot and kill birds and to wring the neck of the hen and the reason he had done so was the violence boiling up inside him. It had not been necessary shooting. He was to blame. But he knew, sensing the presence of the child, that it was over, that he would do no such shooting again. He knew that some evil had been plucked out of him.

He slept.

They sent for him first thing the next morning and he was afraid to face them and when he saw their figures standing at the door, he knew how much they hated and blamed him for the child's death. Halloran's face was flushed with anger and weeping, his eyes flickered like tongues over Nate Twomey, as he took off his cap.

'Get up there. Do what you have to. Get it over with.'

For the second time he followed Amy Halloran up the stairs and at the top she turned to him, standing so close that her breath blew onto his face.

'He blamed me. He said I'd never to let you in and I did. He told me.'

Nate stood still. He felt the bitterness and misery which were directed towards him and wanted to find some way of telling her that things were for the best, that it did not matter that the child had died. He could do nothing, say nothing.

He had expected to feel resentment and anger himself, on seeing the child's body, but it was nothing to him except a comfort. He had known more than this. There was nothing to her. The flesh was wasted and the brittle bones showed through, she measured very little. Her face was rather grave but it held no suffering, the brow was smooth and gleaming, like silk. He would not see her in the carpenter's shop again but that no longer mattered, because he had been with her at the time of her dying and he had all that he wanted or had a right to.

But he grieved for the parents, for Amy Halloran, who watched him, twisting her fingers together, standing at the foot of the bed and for Halloran himself, who would not understand, would not accept. Should he himself not feel as they did? But he did not, for he knew the truth.

He finished his job and put the notebook and pencil away and looked down once more upon the child's body, before going heavily down the stairs.

Halloran was there, waiting for him in the path, his eyes looking swollen and bruised and his mouth working.

He said, 'You came here. You brought it on us. Death. You came here and it killed her. You…'

Nate stood looking at him helplessly, unable to even to shake his head. It was what he had expected. He was a Twomey, he was the coffin-maker. They could not love or trust him.

'You.'

Amy Halloran was there, plucking at her husband's arm, trying to drag him off.

'It was you.'

Then, suddenly, he lunged forward, his eyes wild with pain and rage, and swung his fist into Nate Twomey's face. The blow hit him like a stroke of lightning, he went down, his head spinning, the blood welling up behind his eyes. As he fell, it seemed to him that this was what he had waited for, because of his own anger of the previous day and the lives of the birds he had so ruthlessly and violently taken, so that it was almost a relief when he felt the impact of the ground and pain went like a blade through his body.

He lay for what seemed like hours and then, getting slowly to his feet again, wiping the blood off his face with the back of his hand, he realized that he was alone, that the Hallorans had gone inside the house, had left him. His skull felt as if it would break open. But he was calm. He knew that it was what had been due to him. Because he had loved the child and known of her dying, because he was a Twomey and maimed. He would not have expected anything else and Halloran was grieving, was beside himself with misery and despair. Halloran was not to blame.

The sun shone down on him and his shadow fell behind him, hard and dark against the brightness. He walked back to the carpenter's shop slowly, to begin work on the small coffin, bearing his own silence.

HOW SOON CAN I LEAVE?

The two ladies who lived together were called Miss Bartlett and Miss Roscommon.

Miss Roscommon, the older and stouter of the two, concealed her fear of life behind frank reference to babies and lavatories and the sexing of day-old chicks. It was well known that she had travelled widely as a girl, she told of her walking tours in Greece, and how she had driven an ambulance during the Spanish Civil War.

Miss Bartlett, who was only forty, cultivated shyness and self-effacement, out of which arose her way of leaving muttered sentences to trail off into the air, unfinished. Oh, do not take any notice of anything *I* may say, she meant, it is of no consequence, I am sorry to have spoken…But the sentence drew attention to her, nevertheless.

'What was that?' people said, 'I beg your pardon, I didn't quite catch…Do speak up…' And so, she was forced to repeat herself and they, having brought it upon themselves, were forced to listen. She also protested helplessness in the face of everyday tools. It was Miss Roscommon who peeled all the potatoes and defrosted the refrigerator and opened the tins.

Their house, one of two white bungalows overlooking the bay, was called Tuscany.

When Miss Bartlett had finally come to live with Miss Roscommon, seven years before, each one believed that the step was taken for the good of the other. Miss Bartlett had been living in one of the little stone cottages, opposite the harbour, working through the winter on the stock that she sold, from her front room and on a trestle outside, in summer. From November until March, there were no visitors to Mountsea. Winds and rain scoured the surface of the cliffs and only the lifeboat put out to sea. Miss Roscommon had taken to inviting Miss Bartlett up to the bungalow for meals.

'You should have a shop,' she had begun by saying, loading Miss Bartlett's plate with scones and homemade ginger jam, 'properly equipped and converted. It cannot be satisfactory having to display goods in your living-room. Why have you not thought of taking a shop?'

Miss Bartlett made marquetry pictures of the church, the lighthouse and the harbour, table-lamps out of lobster pots and rocks worked over with shells. She also imported Italian straw baskets and did a little pewter work.

The idea of a shop had come to her, and been at once dismissed, in the first weeks after coming to

Mountsea. She was too timid to take any so definite a step, by establishing herself in a shop, with her name written up on a board outside, was she not establishing herself in the minds of others, as a *shopkeeper*? As a girl, she had been impressed by her mother's constant reference to her as dreamy and artistic, so that she could not possibly now see herself in the role of shopkeeper. Also, by having her name written up on that board, she felt that she would somehow be committing herself to Mountsea, and by doing that, finally abandoning all her hopes of a future in some other place. As a girl, she had looked out at the world, and seen a signpost, with arms pointing in numerous different directions, roads leading here, or here, or there. She had been quite unable to choose which road to take for, having once set out upon any of them, she would thereby be denying herself all the others. And what might I lose, she had thought, what opportunities shall I miss if I make the wrong choice?

So that, in the end, she had never chosen, only drifted through her life from this to that, waking every morning to the expectation of some momentous good fortune dropped in her lap.

'That cottage is damp,' said Miss Roscommon, allowing her persuasions to take on a more personal note, as they got to know one another better. 'I do not think you look after yourself properly. And a place of business should not have to double as a home.'

At first, Miss Bartlett shrank from the hints and

persuasions, knowing herself to be easily swayed, fearful of being swept along on the tide of Miss Roscommon's decision. I am only forty years old, she said, there is plenty of opportunity left for me, I do not have to abandon hope by retreating into middle age, and life with another woman. Though certainly she enjoyed the meals the other cooked; the taste of home-baked pasties and stews and herb-flavoured vegetables.

'I'm afraid that I cannot cook,' she said. 'I live on milk and cheese and oven-baked potatoes. I would not know where to begin in the kitchen.' It did not occur to her that this was any cause for shame, and Miss Roscommon tut-tutted and floured the pastry-board, relieved to have, once again, a sense of purpose brought into her life.

'There were nine of us in the family,' she said, 'and I was the only girl. At the age of seven, I knew how to bake a perfect loaf of bread. I am quite content to be one of the Marthas of this world.'

But I will not go and live there, Miss Bartlett told herself, towards the end of the summer. I am determined to remain independent, my plans are fluid, I have my work, and besides, it would never do, we might not get on well together and then it would be embarrassing for me to have to leave. And people might talk.

Though she knew that they would not, and that it was of her own judgment that she was most afraid, for Mountsea was full of ladies of indeterminate age, sharing houses together.

The winter came, and the cottage was indeed damp. The stone walls struck cold all day and all night, in spite of expensive electric heaters, and Miss Bartlett spent longer and longer afternoons at Tuscany, even taking some of her work up there, from time to time.

At the beginning of December, the first of the bad storms sent waves crashing up over the quayside into the front room.

Of course, Miss Roscommon is lonely, she said now, she has need of me, I should have realized. That type of woman, who appears to be so competent and strong, feels the onset of old age and infirmity more than most, but she cannot say so, cannot give way and confess to human weakness. She bakes me cakes and worries about the dampness in my house because she needs my company and concern for herself.

And so, on Christmas eve, when the second storm filled Miss Bartlett's living-room with water up to the level of the window seat, she allowed herself to be evacuated by the capable Miss Roscommon up to the white bungalow.

'It will not be for good,' she said anxiously, 'when the weather improves, I shall have to go back, there is the business to be thought of.' 'We shall make plans for a proper shop,' said Miss Roscommon firmly, 'I have a little money...'

She filled up a pottery bowl with leek soup, having acquired her faith in its restorative powers when she had set up a canteen at the scene of a mining disaster in the nineteen-twenties.

Miss Bartlett accepted the soup and a chair close to the fire and an electric blanket for her bed, thereby setting the seal on the future pattern of their relationship. By the beginning of February, plans for the shop were made, by mid-March, the work was in hand. There was no longer any talk of her moving, she would sell her goods from the new shop during the summer days, but she would live at Tuscany. The garage was fitted with light, heat and two extra windows, and made into a studio.

'This is quite the best arrangement,' said Miss Roscommon, 'here, you will be properly fed and looked after, I shall see to that.'

Over the seven years that followed, Miss Bartlett came to rely upon her for many more things than the comforts of a well-kept home. It was Miss Roscommon who made all the business arrangements for the new shop, who saw the bank manager, the estate agent and the builder, Miss Roscommon who advised with the orders and the accounts. During the summer seasons, the shop did well, and after three years, at her friend's suggestion, Miss Bartlett started to make pink raffia angels and pot-pourri jars, for the Christmas postal market.

She relaxed, ceased to feel uneasy, and if, from time to time, she did experience a sudden shot of alarm, at seeing herself so well and truly settled, she said, not, 'Where else would I go?' but, 'I am needed here. However would she manage without me? It would be cruel to go.' All the decisions were left to Miss Roscommon. 'You are so much better at these things…' Miss Bartlett said, and drifted away to her studio, a small woman with pastel-coloured flesh.

Perhaps it was her forty-seventh birthday that jolted her into a renewed awareness of the situation. She looked into the mirror on that morning, and saw middle-age settled irrevocably over her features. She was reminded of her dependence upon Miss Roscommon.

I said I would not stay here, she thought, would never have my name written up above a permanent shop, for my plans were to remain fluid. And now it is seven years, and how many opportunities have I missed? How many roads are closed to me?

Or perhaps it was the visit of Miss Roscommon's niece Angela, and her husband of only seven days, one weekend in early September.

'I shall do a great deal of baking,' Miss Roscommon said, 'for they will certainly stay to tea. We shall have cheese scones and preserves and a layer cake.'

'I did not realize that you had a niece.'

Miss Roscommon rose from the table heavily, for she had put on weight, over the seven years. There had also been some suspicion about a cataract in her left eye, another reason why Miss Bartlett told herself she could not leave her.

'She is my youngest brother's child. I haven't seen her since she was a baby.'

Miss Bartlett nodded and wandered away from the breakfast table, not liking to ask why there had been no wedding invitation. Even after seven years, Miss Roscommon kept some of her secrets, there were subjects upon which she simply did not speak, though Miss Bartlett had long ago bared her own soul.

The niece Angela, and her new husband, brought a slab of wedding cake, which was put to grace the centre of the table, on a porcelain stand.

'And this,' said Miss Roscommon triumphantly, '*this* is my friend, Miss Mary Bartlett.' For Miss Bartlett had hung behind in the studio for ten minutes after their arrival, out of courtesy and because it was always something of a strain for her to meet new people.

'Mary is very shy, very retiring,' her own mother had always said, 'she is artistic, you see, she lives in her own world.' Her tone had always been proud and Miss Bartlett had therefore come to see her own failure as a mark of distinction. Her shyness had been cultivated, readily admitted to.

The niece and her husband sat together on the sofa, a little flushed and self-conscious in new clothes. Seeing them there, Miss Bartlett realized for the first time that no young people had ever been inside the bungalow, since her arrival. But it was more than their youthfulness which struck her, there was an air of suppressed excitement about them, a glitter, they emanated pride in the satisfaction of the flesh.

Miss Roscommon presided over a laden tea-table, her face still flushed from the oven.

'And Miss Bartlett is very clever,' she told them, 'she makes beautiful things. You must go down to the shop and see them, buy something for your new home.'

'You make things?' said Angela, through a mouthful of shortbread, 'what sort of things?'

Miss Bartlett made a little gesture of dismissal with her hand. Oh, not very much really, nothing at all exciting. Just a few little...I'm sure you wouldn't...' She let her voice trail off, but it was Miss Roscommon and not the niece Angela who took her up on it.

'Now that is just nonsense,' she said firmly. 'There is no virtue in this false modesty, I have told you before. Of course Angela will like your things, why should she not? Plenty of visitors do, and there is nothing to be ashamed of in having a talent.'

'I wore a hand-embroidered dress,' said the niece Angela, 'for my wedding.'

Miss Bartlett watched her, and watched the new husband, whose eyes followed Angela's slim hand as it moved over to the cake plate and back, and up into her mouth. Their eyes met and shone with secrets, across the table. Miss Bartlett's stomach moved a little, with fear and excitement. She felt herself to be within touching distance of some very important piece of knowledge.

'Do you help with this shop, then -?' asked the husband though without interest.

'Oh, no! Well, here and there with the accounts and so forth, because Mary doesn't understand any of that, she is such a dreamer! No, no, that is not my job, that is not what keeps me so busy. My job is to look after Mary, of course. I took that upon myself quite some time ago, when I saw that I was needed. She is such a silly girl, she lives in a world of her own and if I were not here to worry about her meals and her comforts, she would starve, I assure you, simply starve.'

'Oh, I don't think I really…'

'Of course you would,' said Miss Roscommon. 'Now let me have your cup to be filled.'

The young couple exchanged another glance of comprehension and amusement. How dare you, thought Miss Bartlett, almost in tears with anger and frustration, at being so looked upon and judged and misunderstood. What do you know of it, how can you sit there so smugly? It is because you are young and know nothing. It is all very well for you.

'All the same,' said the niece Angela, sitting back in her chair, 'it's nice to be looked after, I must say.'

She smiled like a cat.

'Yes, that has always been my role in life, that is my talent,' said Miss Roscommon, 'to do all the looking after.' She leaned over and patted Miss Bartlett on the hand. 'She is my responsibility now, you see,' she told them confidently. 'My little pussy-cat.'

Miss Bartlett pushed the hand away and got to her feet, her face flushed with shame and annoyance. 'What a foolish thing to say! Of course I am not, how very silly you make me look. I am a grown woman, I am quite capable of looking after myself.'

Miss Roscommon, not in the least discomfited, only began to pour the tea dregs into a slop basin, smiling.

When they were about to leave, Miss Bartlett said, 'I will walk down the hill with you, and we shall drop in for a minute at the shop. Yes, I insist…But not for you to buy anything. You must choose a wedding present from my stock, it is the very least I can do.' For she wanted to keep them with her longer, to be seen walking in their company down the hill away from the bungalow, wanted to be on their side.

'You will need a warm coat, it is autumn now the evenings are drawing in. Take your mohair.'

'Oh, leave me, leave me, do not *fuss*.' And Miss Bartlett walked to the end of the gravelled drive, while the niece and her new husband made their good-byes.

'I am afraid it is all she has to worry over nowadays,' she said hastily, the moment they had joined her. 'It gives her pleasure, I suppose, to do all that clucking round and I have not the heart to do anything but play along, keep up appearances. If it were not for me, she would be so lonely. Of course, I have had to give up a good deal of my own life, on that account.'

The niece Angela took her husband's arm. 'It must

be very nice and comfortable for you there,' she said, 'all the same.'

Miss Bartlett turned her face away and looked out to sea. Another winter she thought, and I am now forty-seven years old. You do not understand.

She detained them in the shop for as long as possible, fetching out special items from the stock room and taking time over the wrapping paper. Let me be with you, she wanted to say, let me be on your side, for do you not see that I still have many opportunities left, I am not an old woman, I know about the world and the ways of modern life? Take me with you.

But when they had gone she stood in the darkening shop and saw that they had already gone and dismissed her, that she did not belong with them and there was no hope left. She sat on the stool beside the till and wept, for the injustice of the world and the weakness of her own nature. I have become what I always dreaded becoming, she said, everything has slipped through my fingers.

And for all of it, after a short time, she began to blame Miss Roscommon. She has stifled me, she thought, she preys upon me, I am treated as her child, her toy, her *pussy-cat*, she has humiliated me and fed off my dependence and the fact that I have always been so sensitive. She is a wicked woman. And then she said, *but I do not have to stay with her.* Fortified by the truth of this new realization, Miss Bartlett blew her nose, and walked back up the hill to Tuscany.

*

'You cannot leave,' said Miss Roscommon, 'what non-sense, of course you cannot. You have nowhere else to go and besides, in ten days' time we set off for our holiday in Florence.'

'You will set off. I am afraid my plans have now changed.' Miss Bartlett could not now bear the thought of being seen with her friend in al the museums and art galleries of Florence, discussing the paintings in loud, knowledgeable voices and eating wholemeal sandwiches out of neat little greaseproof bags, speaking very slowly to the Italians. This year Miss Roscommon must go alone. She did not allow herself to think of how, or whether she would enjoy herself. We are always hearing of how intrepid she was as a girl, she thought. Then let her be intrepid again.

Aloud, she said, 'I am going back to live at the cottage.' For she had kept it on, and rented it to summer visitors.

Miss Roscommon turned herself, and her darning, a little more towards the light. 'You are being very foolish,' she said mildly. 'But I understand why, it is your age, of course.'

Appalled, Miss Bartlett went through to her room, and began to throw things furiously, haphazardly, into a suitcase. I am my own mistress, she said, a grown-up woman with years ahead of me, it is time for me to be firm. I have pandered to her long enough.

The following day, watched by Miss Roscommon,

she moved back down the hill to the cottage. She would, she decided, stay there for a while, give herself time to get accustomed, and to gather all of her things around her again, and then she would look out and make plans, take steps towards her new life.

That evening, hearing the wind around her own four walls, she said, I have escaped. Though she woke in the night and was aware of being entirely alone in the cottage, of not being able to hear the loud breathing of Miss Roscommon in the room next door.

She expected the Italian holiday to be cancelled, on some pretext, and was astonished when Miss Roscommon left, on the appointed day and alone. Miss Bartlett took the opportunity of going up to Tuscany and fetching some more of her things down, work from the studio to keep her busy in the evening, and during the days, too, for now it was October and few people came into the shop.

Here I am, she said, twisting the raffia angels and winding ribbon around the pot-pourris, etching her gift cards, here I am, living my own life and making my own decisions. She wanted to invite someone down to stay, someone young, so that she could be seen and approved of, but there was no one. A search through all the drawers and cupboards at the bungalow did not yield her the address of the niece Angela. She would have sent a little note, with a Christmas gift, to tell of her removal, prove her independence.

Miss Roscommon returned from Italy, looked

rather tired and not very suntanned. She came in with a miniature plaster copy of a Donatello statue, and some fine art post-cards. Miss Bartlett made tea, and the conversation was very stilted.

'You are not warm enough here,' said Miss Roscommon, 'I will send down some extra blankets.'

'Oh no, thank you. Please don't do that.'

But the following day the blankets, and a Dutch apple pie, arrived with the butcher's boy.

Miss Bartlett bought huge slabs of cheese and eggs, which she could boil quite well, and many potatoes, and ate them off her knee while she read detective stories through the long evenings. She thought that she might buy a television set for company, though she was busy too, with the postal orders for Christmas. When all this is over, she told herself, that is when I shall start looking about me and making my plans. She thought of all the things she might have done as a girl, the studio in London and the woodblock engravings for the poetry press, the ballet company for whom she might have been asked to do some ethereal costume designs. She read in a newspaper of a woman who had started her own firm, specializing in computer management, at the age of fifty and was now rather wealthy, wholly respected in a man's world. Miss Bartlett looked at herself in the mirror. I am only forty-seven, she said.

In her white bungalow, lonely and lacking a sense of purpose, Miss Roscommon waited.

On November the seventh, the first of the storms

came, and Miss Bartlett sat in her back room and heard the wind and the crashing of the sea, terrified. The next morning, she saw that part of the pierhead had broken away. Miss Roscommon sent down a note, with a meat pasty, via the butcher's boy.

'I am worried about you,' she wrote, 'you cannot be looking after yourself, and I know that it is damp in that cottage. Your room here is ready for you at any time.'

Miss Bartlett tore the note up and threw the pasty away, but she thought of the warm bed, the fires and soft sofas at Tuscany.

Two days later, when the gales began again, Miss Roscommon came herself, and hammered at the door of the cottage, but Miss Bartlett hid upstairs, behind a cheval mirror, until she went away. This time, there was no note, only a thermos flask of lentil soup on the doorstep.

She is suffocating me, thought Miss Bartlett, I cannot bear all these unwanted attentions, I only wish to be left alone. It is a poor thing if a woman of her age and resources can find nothing else to occupy her, nothing else to live for. But in spite of herself, she drank the soup, and the taste of it, the smell of the steam rising up into her face reminded her of all the meals at Tuscany, the winter evenings spent happily sitting beside the fire.

When the storms came again, another section of the pier broke away, the lifeboat put out to sea and

sank with all hands, and the front room of Miss
Bartlett's cottage was flooded, rain broke in through a
rent in the roof. She lay all night, too terrified by the
roaring of the wind and seas to get out of bed and do
anything about it, only whimpering a little with cold
and fright, remembering how close the cottage came to
the water, how vulnerable she was.

As a child, she had been afraid of all storms, gales
and thunder and cloudbursts drumming on the roof,
and her mother had understood, wrapped her in a
blanket and taken her into her own bed.

'It is because you have such a vivid imagination,'
she had said, 'you feel things that the other, ordinary
little children, cannot ever feel.' And so nothing had
been done to conquer this praiseworthy fear of storms.

Now, I am alone, thought Miss Bartlett, there is no
one, my mother is dead, and who is there to shelter
and understand me? A flare rocket, sent up from the
sinking lifeboat, lit up the room faintly for a second,
and then she knew who there was, and that everything
would be all right. On the stormy nights, Miss
Roscommon always got up and made sandwiches and
milky hot drinks, brought them to her as she lay awake
in bed, and they would sit reading nice magazines, in
the gentle circle of the bedside lamp.

I have been very foolish, Miss Bartlett thought, and
heard herself saying it out loud, humbly, to Miss
Roscommon. A very foolish, selfish woman, I do not
deserve to have you as a friend.

She did not take very much with her up the hill on the following morning, only a little hand case and some raffia work. The rest could follow her, and it would be better to arrive like that, it would be a real indication of her helplessness.

The landscape was washed very clean and bare and pale, but the sea churned and moved within itself, angry and battleship grey. In the summer, Miss Bartlett thought, refreshed again by the short walk, it will be time to think again, for I am not committing myself to any permanent arrangements and things will have to be rather different now, I will not allow myself to be treated as a plaything, that must be understood. For she had forgotten, in the cold, clear morning, the terrors of the previous night.

She wondered what to do, ring the bell or knock or simply open the back door into the kitchen, where Miss Roscommon would be working, and stand there, case in hand, waiting to be forgiven. Her heart beat a little faster. Tuscany was very settled and reassuring in its low, four-square whiteness on top of the hill. Miss Bartlett knocked timidly at the blue kitchen door.

It was some time before she gave up knocking and ringing, and simply went in. Tuscany was very quiet.

She found her in the living-room, lying crumpled awkwardly on the floor, one of her legs twisted underneath her. Her face was a curious, flat colour, like the inside of a raw potato. Miss Bartlett drew back the curtains. The clock had stopped just before midnight, almost twelve hours ago.

For a moment, she stood there, still holding her little case, in the comfortable, chintzy room, and then she dropped down on to her knees, and took the head of Miss Roscommon into her lap and, rocking and rocking, cradling it like a child, Miss Bartlett wept.

THE BADNESS WITHIN HIM

The night before, he had knelt beside his bed and prayed for a storm, an urgent, hysterical prayer. But even while he prayed he had known that there could be no answer, because of the badness within him, a badness which was living and growing like a cancer. So that he was not surprised to draw back the curtains and see the pale, glittering mist of another hot day. But he was angry. He did not want the sun and the endless stillness and brightness, the hard-edged shadows and the endless gleam of the sea. They came to this place every summer, they had been here, now, since the first of August, and they had one week more left. The sun had shone from the beginning. He wondered how he would bear it.

At the breakfast table, Jess sat opposite to him and her hand kept moving up to rub at the sunburned skin which was peeling off her nose.

'Stop *doing* that.'

Jess looked up slowly. This year for the first time, Col felt the difference in age between them, he saw that Jess was changing, moving away from him to join the adults. She was almost fourteen.

'What if the skin doesn't grow again? What then? You look awful enough now.'

She did not reply, only considered him for a long time, before returning her attention to the cereal plate. After a moment, her hand went up again to the peeling skin.

Col thought, I hate it here. I hate it. *I hate it.* And he clenched his fist under cover of the table until the fingernails hurt him, digging into his palm. He had suddenly come to hate it, and the emotion frightened him. It was the reason why he had prayed for the storm, to break the pattern of long, hot still days and waken the others out of their contentment, to change things. Now, everything was as it had always been in the past and he did not want the past, he wanted the future.

But the others were happy here, they slipped into the gentle, lazy routine of summer as their feet slipped into sandals, they never grew bored or angry or irritable, never quarrelled with one another. For days now Co had wanted to quarrel.

How had he ever been able to bear it? And he cast about, in his frustration, for some terrible event, as he felt the misery welling up inside him at the beginning of another day.

I hate it here. He hated the house itself, the chintz curtains and covers bleached by the glare of the sun, and the crunch of sand like sugar spilled in the hall and along the tiled passages, the windows with peeling paint always open on to the garden, and the porch cluttered with sandshoes and buckets and deckchairs, the muddle and shabbiness of it all.

They all came down to breakfast at different times, and ate slowly and talked of nothing, made no plans, for that was what the holiday was for, a respite from plans and time-tables.

Fay pulled out the high-chair and sat her baby down next to Col.

'You can help him with his egg.'

'Do I have to?'

Fay stared at him, shocked that anyone should not find her child desirable.

'Do help, Col, you know the baby can't manage by himself.'

'Col's got a black dog on his shoulder.'

'Shut up.'

'A perfectly enormous, coal black, monster of a dog!'

He kicked out viciously at his sister under the table. Jess began to cry.

'Now, Col, you are to apologize please.' His mother looked paler than ever, exhausted. Fay's baby dug fingers of toast down deeper and deeper into the yolk of egg.

'You hurt me, you hurt me.'

He looked out of the window. The sea was a thin, glistening line. Nothing moved. Today would be the same as yesterday and all the other days – nothing would happen, nothing would change. He felt himself itching beneath his skin.

They had first come here when he was three years old. He remembered how great the distance had seemed as he jumped from rock to rock on the beach, how he had scarcely been able to stretch his leg across and balance. Then, he had stood for minute after minute feeling the damp ribs of sand under his feet. He had been enchanted with everything. He and Jess had collected buckets full of sea creatures from the rock pools and put them into a glass aquarium in the scullery, though always the starfish and anemones and limpets died after a few captive days. They had taken jam jars up on to West Cliff and walked along, at the hottest part of the day, looking for chrysalides on the grass stalks. The salt had dried in white tide marks around their brown legs, and Col had reached down and rubbed some off with his finger and then licked it. In the sun lounge the moths and butterflies had swollen and cracked open their frail, papery coverings and crept out like babies from the womb, and he and Jess had sat up half the night by the light of moon or candle watching them.

And so it had been every year and often, in winter or windy spring in London, he remembered it all, the smell of the sunlit house and the feeling of the warm sea lapping against his thighs and the line of damp woollen bathing shorts outside the open back door. It was another world, but it was still there, and when every summer came they would return to it, things would be the same.

Yet now, he wanted to do some violence in this house, he wanted an end to everything. He was afraid of himself.

'Col's got a black dog on his shoulder!'

So he left them and went for a walk on his own, over the track beside the gorse bushes and up – onto the coarse grass of the sheep field behind West Cliff. The mist was rolling away, the sea was white-gold at the edges, creaming back. On the far side of the field there were poppies.

He lay down and pressed his face and hands into the warm turf until he could smell the soil beneath and gradually, he felt the warmth of the sun on his back and it soothed him.

In the house, his mother and sisters left the break-fast table and wandered upstairs to find towels and sunhats and books, content that this day should be the same as all the other days, wanting the summer to last. And later, his father would join them for the weekend, coming down on the train from London, he would discard the blue city suit and emerge, hairy and thickly fleshed, to lie on a rug and play with Fay's baby, rounding off the family circle.

By eleven it was hotter than it had been all summer, the dust rose in soft clouds when a car passed down the lane to the village, and did not settle again, and the leaves of the hedges were mottled and dark, the birds went quiet. Col felt his own anger like a pain tightening around his head. He went up to the house and the sunlight fell in a straight, hard beam across his bed and on to the printed page, making his eyes hurt.

When he was younger he had liked this room, he had sometimes dreamed of it when he was in London. He had collected shells and small pebbles and laid them out in careful piles, and hung up a bladder-wrack on a nail by the open window, had brought books from home about fossils and shipwrecks and propped them on top of the painted wooden chest. But now it felt too small, it stifled him, it was a childish room, a pale, dead room in which nothing ever happened and nothing would change.

After a while he heard his father's taxi come up the drive.

'Col, watch what you're doing near the baby, you'll get sand in his eyes.'

'Col, if you want to play this game with us, do, but otherwise go away, if you can't keep still, you're just spoiling it.'

'Col, why don't you build a sandcastle or something?'

He stood looking down at them all, at his mother and Fay playing cards in the shade of the green parasol, and his father lying on his back, black-haired chest shiny with oil and his nostrils flaring in and out as he breathed, at Jess, who had begun to build the sandcastle for the baby, instead of him. She had her hair tied back in bunches and the freckles had come out even more thickly across her cheekbones, she might have been eleven years old. But she was almost fourteen, she had gone away from him.

'Col, don't kick sand around like that, it's flying everywhere. Why don't you go and have a swim? Why can't you find something to do? I do so dislike you just hovering over us like that.'

Jess had filled a small bucket with water from the rock pool, and now she bent down and began to pour it carefully into the moat. It splashed on to her bare feet and she wriggled her toes. Fay's baby bounced up and down with interest and pleasure in the stream of water and the crenellated golden castle.

Col kicked again more forcefully. The clods of sand hit the tower of the castle sideways, and, as it fell, crumbled the edges off the other towers and broke open the surrounding wall, so that everything toppled into the moat, clouding the water.

Jess got to her feet, scarlet in the face, ready to hit out at him.

'I hate you. *I hate you.*'

'Jess…'

'He wants to spoil everything, look at him, he doesn't want anyone else to enjoy themselves, he just wants to sulk and…I hate him.'

Col thought, I am filled with evil, there is no hope

for me. For he felt himself completely taken over by the badness within him.

'*I hate you.*'

He turned away from his sister's wild face and her mouth which opened and shut over and over again to shout her rejection of him, turned away from them all and began to walk towards the cave at the far side of the cove. Above them were the cliffs.

Three-quarters of the way up there was a ledge around which the gannets and kittiwakes nested. He had never climbed up as high as this before. There were tussocks of grass, dried and bleached bone-pale by the sea winds, and he clung on to them and to the bumps of chalky rock. Flowers grew, pale wild scabious and cliff buttercups, and when he rested, he touched his face to them. Above his head, the sky was enamel blue. The sea birds watched him with eyes like beads. As he climbed higher, the wash of the sea and the voices of those on the beach receded. When he reached the ledge, he got his breath and then sat down cautiously, legs dangling over the edge. There was just enough room for him. The surface of the cliff was hot on his back. He was not at all afraid.

His family were like insects down on the sand, little shapes of colour dotted about at random. Jess was a pink shape, the parasol was bottle-glass green, Fay and Fay's baby were yellow. For most of the time they were still, but once they all clustered around the parasol to look at something and then broke away again, so that it was like a dance. The other people on the beach were quite separate, each family kept to itself. Out beyond the curve of the cliff the beach lay like a ribbon bounded by the tide, which did not reach as far as the cove except in the storms of winter. They had never been here during the winter.

When Col opened his eyes again his head swam for a moment. Everything was the same. The sky was think and clear. The sun shone. If he had gone to sleep he might have tipped over and fallen forwards. The thought did not frighten him.

But all was not the same, for now he saw his father had left the family group and was padding down towards the sea. The black hairs curled up the backs of his legs and the soles of his feet were brownish pink as they turned up one after the other.

Col said, do I like my father? And thought about it. And did not know.

Fay's baby was crawling after him, its lemon-coloured behind stuck up in the air.

Now, Col half-closed his eyes, so that air and sea and sand shimmered, merging together.

Now, he felt rested, no longer angry, he felt above it all.

Now, he opened his eyes again and saw his father striding into the water, until it reached up to his chest: then he flopped onto his belly and floated for a moment, before beginning to swim.

Col thought, perhaps I am ill and *that* is the bad-ness within me.

But if he had changed, the others had changed too. Since Fay had married and had the baby and gone to live in Berkshire, she was different, she fussed more, was concerned with the details of things, she spoke to them all a trifle impatiently. And his mother was so languid. And Jess – Jess did not want his company.

Now he saw his father's dark head bobbing up and down quite a long way out to sea, but as he watched, sitting on the high cliff ledge in the sun, the bobbing stopped – began again – an arm came up and waved, as if it were uncertain of its direction.

Col waved back.

The sun was burning the top of his head.

Fay and Fay's baby and Jess had moved in around the parasol again, their heads were bent together. Col thought, we will never be the same with one another, the ties of blood make no difference, we are separate people now. And then he felt afraid of such truth. Father's waving stopped abruptly, he bobbed and dis-appeared, bobbed up again.

The sea was still as glass.

Col saw that his father was drowning.

In the end, a man from the other side of the beach went running down to the water's edge and another to where the family were grouped around the parasol. Col looked at the cliff, falling away at his feet. He closed his eyes and turned around slowly and then got down on his hands and knees and began to feel for a foothold, though not daring to look. His head was hot and throbbing.

By the time he reached the bottom, they were bringing his father's body. Col stood on the shadow of the cliff and shivered and smelled the dank, cave smell behind him. His mother and Fay and Jess stood in a line, very erect, like Royalty at the cenotaph, and in Fay's arms the baby was still as a doll.

Everyone else kept away. Though Col could see that they made half-gestures, raised an arm or turned a head, occasionally took an uncertain step forward, before retreating again.

Eventually he wondered if they had forgotten about him. The men dripped water off their arms and shoulders as they walked and the sea ran off the body, too, in a thin, steady stream.

Nobody spoke to him about the cliff climb. People only spoke of baths and hot drinks and telephone messages, scarcely looking at one another as they did so, and the house was full of strangers moving from room to room.

In bed, he lay stiffly under the tight sheets and looked towards the window where the moon shone. He thought, it is my fault. I prayed for some terrible happening and the badness within me made it come about. I am punished. For this was a change greater than any he could have imagined.

When he slept he dreamed of drowning, and woke early, just at dawn. Outside the window, a dove grey mist muffled everything. He felt the cold linoleum under his feet and the dampness in his nostrils. When he reached the bottom of the stairs he saw at once that the door of the sun parlour was closed. He stood for a moment outside, listening to the creaking of the house, imagining all of them in their beds, his mother lying alone. He was afraid. He turned the brass door-knob and went slowly in.

There were windows on three sides of the room, long and uncurtained, with a view of the sea, but now there was only the fog pressing up against the panes, the curious stillness. The floor was polished and partly covered with rush matting and in the ruts of this the sand of the summer past had gathered and lay, soft and gritty, the room smelled of seaweed. On the walls, the sepia photographs of his great-grandfather the Captain, and his naval friends and their ships. He had always liked this room. When he was small, he had sat here with his mother on warm, August evenings, drinking his mug of milk, and the smell of stocks came in to them from the open windows. The deckchairs had always been in a row outside on the terrace, empty at the end of the day. He stepped forward.

They had put his father's body on the trestle, dressed in a shirt and covered with a sheet and a rug. His head was bare and lay on a cushion, and the hands, with the black hair over their backs, were folded together. Now, he was not afraid. His father's skin was oddly pale and shiny. He stared, trying to feel some sense of loss and sorrow. He had watched his father drown, though for a long time he had not believed it, the water had been so entirely calm. Later, he had heard them talking of a heart attack, and then he had understood better why this strong barrel of a man, down that day from the City, should have been so suddenly sinking, sinking.

The fog horn sounded outside. Then, he knew that the change had come, knew that the long, hot summer was at an end, and that his childhood had ended too, that they would never come to this house again. He knew, finally, the power of the badness within him and because of that, standing close to his father's body, he wept.

RED AND GREEN BEADS

All afternoon the Curé had been walking and it was after five o'clock as he came down the slope towards the village and met Albert Piguet. A hundred years ago all the land on both sides of the valley had belonged to the Piguets. The Curé remembered the old man sitting on a walnut stump outside his back door, his head nodding forwards and a thin trickle of rheum wetting the grey stubbled chin. The dog had always been lying at his feet, Lascar, a thin vulpine creature with the pointed head and arched back of a greyhound. Nobody dared to touch Lascar save the old man.

But that was fifty years ago, when he had come here to his first parish. Then, he used to stride the length and breadth of it, feeling a kind of boundless excitement, for in those days he had known what he believed, what life was all about, he had been both devout and ambitious. For many years, the parishioners had been suspicious of him.

Old man Piguet had remembered three of his predecessors and talked a great deal about them so that when Curé Begnac looked up their names in the parish registers he felt close to them. Often he walked in the graveyard opposite the church and stood for a moment before each of their three plain headstones.

The Piguet land was broken up now, they had had misfortune, sickness and accidents and deaths, since before the old man had died and gradually they had had to sell of this and that field to the other farmers around. Now they owned only two, together with a few vines and an orchard. And they continued to be unlucky, both in the business and in the family. They had sold the red-tiled farmhouse and moved to a cottage which had once been let out to a man they employed. Albert's latest brother had been killed falling off a cart and Albert himself was bent and grey before his time, his eyes weary in a sallow face.

He was not yet fifty.

The Curé stopped and watched him mending two of the bird scarers. Very early that morning, as he was going up the church path to say Mass, he had seen Albert's youngest boy slipping up towards the wood, where he would search for the big cepes for an hour, before going to school. As soon as Piguets walked now they must work. All except Marcel, who only counted his string of red and green beads.

Now, Albert saw the Curé and stood up, putting a hand round for a moment to his aching back. The sky was clear, bright blue with streaks of mulberry cloud over to the west. The gnats were gathering.

'Curé.' Albert watched the old man make his way along the field track. He is old, he thought – well, we are all old. But the priest seemed to have shriveled and dried out, like a branch without sap, the shape of his skull was revealed under the thin coating of flesh.

They stood together beside the hedge and talked about the harvest and the weather and the illness of Madame Curveillers at the Chateau.

'I married them,' Curé Begnac said reflectively. For all that day, the past had shadowed him.

'So you did. I was a boy but I remember it all right – I climbed the church wall and threw a handful of petals. They'd gone damp and started to brown. I'd been clutching them so long but I threw them just the same. That was a day !'

'How is Amelie?'

'The same. Her leg troubles her. She dreads the bad weather coming. And her father is worse, madder than ever. We'll have to try and get him down here for the winter, somehow or other, he can't be left in that hovel of his, though Lord knows there's little enough room with us.'

'I must go and see him, but…'

'But he won't thank you. I know. Rude old devil.'

There was a silence then, during which the Curé might have asked about Marcel. He had not seen the boy for several days. He wondered if he had been told about Madame Curveiller's illness and if he understood. She was the only person who took any notice of

Marcel; she talked to him sometimes, as they came out of mass. To him and to no one else.

But what could Albert say? 'The same. Always the same…' When he got back home, then was enough time to be reminded of the boy. The Curé had tried to bring him round to a change of attitude but he knew now that he had tried in the wrong way. He was ashamed to remember how he had been, raw and tactless and over-confident that he knew what was right. It had taken fifty years for him to learn something about acceptance. And silence.

Piguet said, 'Everything's the same,' and scratched his leg with the other, mud-caked boot.

And so it was. And yet, not the same at all. Little by little, the character of the soil altered, trees grew and were felled, changing the contours of the woodlands. Last winter the river had flooded into a field which had never been fully drained, so that now the pasture was a marsh. One of Piguet's cows had drowned in it. That was the kind of thing which happened to them. The Curé listened to Piguet's confessions of resentment and grievance against God. Why do these things happen to us? Why always to us? And could not answer.

On the night that his small daughter had died, Albert had stood in the presbytery path and cursed, and then wept, beating his fists again and again upon the crumbling stone wall.

The parish register was full of births and marriages and

deaths and many of the deaths were untimely .Nothing changed. Everything changed. But one thing which never changed was the distance they set between themselves and the Curé. So, Piguet stood now waiting for him to speak again or to shake hands and leave. In their minds, the priest, like the blind, the dumb and the mad, inhabited some special place, was somehow different and set apart. The Curé wished it was not so. He did not want to be cut off from the people among whom he had lived for so long. He looked at them when they took the communion wafer, when he held their infants for baptism and stood over the coffins of the dead, and felt nothing but loneliness, a desire to throw out his arms and cry to them. But when they asked him questions, he could no longer answer.

He patted Albert on the shoulder and walked away.

That night Madame Curveillers died. Robert's boy came to the presbytery at ten o'clock with an urgent message for the Curé. He wished that he could mourn her, if only because no one else would – she had been a widow for fifteen years and was childless. One-eyed Gaston and his wife, the housekeeper, stood together in the shadowy hall waiting for news, but when it came they did not weep. And to Curé Begnac, death now seemed a more natural condition than life.

'Are you distressed?' asked the doctor, who was young and suspicious of the church.

'She was very old.'

'Certainly. With respect, you are old. But I asked if you were distressed.'

'Why?'

'She was an old friend of yours. There can't be many of those left now.'

Friend? No. For how much had Madame Curveillers and he known one another, below the surface politeness? He had heard her confession once a week for forty years. He had taken the communion to her when she had become house and then bed-bound. But she had not been his friend. None of them were.

'Was she a good woman?'

The Curé stopped in the middle of the flight of stone stairs. He realized that he could not answer, not so much because the matter was confidential, as because he no longer knew – perhaps had never known – what 'good' was. If they asked him to define it, he could not.

'I daresay she was like the rest of us,' Doctor Domecq said. 'The usual mixture.'

'Perhaps.'

He left the house. But in the middle of the path and when still a mile from home, he stopped again and heard the night sounds, the faint silky rush of the air, the creak of cherry and chestnut trees.

What was 'good'? He did not know. He felt suddenly afraid.

*

Marie had left him some cold supper and he drank a glass of wine. He was shivering. The fire glowed still and sparked up when he threw on another log.

So, Madame was dead. But it was not this which had so upset and confused him. He tried to read his breviary but his eyes smarted, tried to pray, but could only think that he had not been able to answer the question.

He slept. And dreamed of the night he had been fetched to the Piguet cottage after the birth of Marcel.

The great bed had looked out of place in this poky, low-ceilinged room. A fire burned and Albert Piguet had been sitting beside it, the little girl on his lap. Amelie lay in the bed, her hair streaked dark with sweat, her eyes feverish. The Curé went over and touched her hand.

'Amelie..'

The fire had hissed as Albert spat into it disgustedly. Amelie had given him a look of exhaustion. And anger. She was a proud, rather hard woman, daughter of Nouvert, who lived by trapping and skinning animals.

Now, she gestured to the cot which stood in the shadow of the bed. She did not look at it herself.

'You have a son?'

There was silence then, save for the shifting of the fire and the sound of the small girl as she murmured to her father.

The Curé leaned over and touched the baby's face.

Then Albert had raised his voice across the cramped, hot room.

'Pull back the covers, Father – go on, see it for yourself. Look.'

The small body was twisted to one side. There was a lump on the back and both legs ended just below the knee.

'See what we are blessed with !'

That winter, the little girl died.

'Why not him?' Albert Piguet had shouted. 'Why couldn't he be the one to die?'

To Curé Begnac that night for the first time in his life there had been no sense in things as there was sense now in the death of old Madame Curveillers, who had been old and ill and lonely.

The fire was out. He loosened his cramped limbs and went slowly to bed. In his mind, still, was the question he could not answer.

Madame Curveiller's funeral was on the Tuesday. The weather was grey and dank and there were few mourners. The Curé felt old and ill and confused. His life seemed to have been lived in complete ignorance of truth.

The next morning was even colder. If the weather continued like this the grapes would rot before they were ready to be harvested and men like Piguet would lose the money which was to see them through the winter.

At the entrance to the graveyard the Curé stopped. Someone was there, but it was too early for Madame Machaut, who tended the graves and swept the paths clear of leaves.

He went on through the gateway.

Marcel Piguet was squatting beside Madame Curveiller's freshly mounded grave and scrabbling gently in the soil with his hands. The hunch on his back had grown with him and his head had sunk down. He wore two wooden half-legs, the leather straps going over his shoulders, and he walked in a cumbersome fashion on crutches. He was twenty now, a large boy but with a child's soft-skinned and hairless face. In the village some were afraid of him and the children ran after him shouting, they imitated him, hopping on one leg. Marcel never minded. He watched them and clapped when he thought they had got it right.

When he heard the footsteps now he turned.

'Marcel? What are you doing? This is Madame Curveiller's grave.'

But the boy only got up then, patted the loose soil back into place and taking the old priest's hand, pulled him away. They walked together back to the cottage.

'Well, he goes,' Amelie said, shrugging. 'I don't know where. I can't be forever watching him. He's old enough isn't he? He'll come to no harm I suppose.'

Marcel smiled and tried to embrace her.

When Curé Begnac got back to the grave he uncovered the small pile of soil, and found the string of red and green beads. Marcel always had them somewhere about him, in his hand or his pocket, they seemed to be a comfort. He would finger them and count them and sometimes touch them to his face, smiling. What he would never do was let them go. Until now, when he had brought them to the grave of Madame Curveillers.

The Curé bent down and re-buried them and for a moment did not know how he would get up again, his legs were so stiff and painful. But he managed it, and walked home.

It was raining. He was glad to reach his chair. Marie had only just lit the fire and the room was cold. He sat there for a long time, thinking about Madame Curveillers and Marcel Piguet, and Marcel's gift of the red and green beads, which had given him, at last, the answer to his question.

He outlived the old lady by less than a couple of weeks.

FARTHING HOUSE

I have never told you any of this before – I have never told anyone, and indeed, writing it down and sealing it up in an envelope to be read at some future date may still not count as 'telling'. But I shall feel better for it, I am sure of that. Now it has all come back to me, I do not want to let it go again, I must set it down. It is true, and for that very reason you must not hear it just now. You will be prey to enough anxieties and fancies without my adding ghosts to them; the time before the birth of a child one is so very vulnerable. I daresay that it has made me vulnerable too, that this has brought the event to mind. I began to be restless several weeks ago. I was burning the last of the leaves. It was a most beautiful day, clear and cold and blue and a few of them were swirling down as I raked and piled. And then a light wind blew suddenly across the grass, scuttling the leaves and making the wood smoke drift towards me, and as I caught the smell of it, that most poignant, melancholy, nostalgic of all smells, something that had been drifting on the edges of my consciousness blurred and insubstantial, came into focus, and in a rush I remembered... It was as though a door had been opened on to the past, and I had stepped through and gazed at what I saw there again. I saw the house, the drive sweeping up to it, the countryside around it, on that late November afternoon, saw the red sun setting behind the beech copse, beyond the rising, brown fields, saw the bonfire the gardener had left to smoulder on gently by itself, and the thin pale smoke coiling up from its heart. I was there, all over again. I went in a daze into the house, made some tea, and sat, still in my old, outdoor clothes at the kitchen table, as it went quite dark outside the window, and I let myself go back to that day, and the nights that followed, watched it all unfold again, remembered. So that it was absolutely clear in my mind when the newspaper report appeared, a week later. I was going to see Aunt Addy. It was November, and she had been at a place called Farthing House since the New Year, but it was only now that I had managed to get away and make the two-hundred-mile journey to visit her.

We had written, of course, and spoken on the telephone, and so far as I could tell she sounded happy. Yes, they were very nice people, she said, and yes, it was such a lovely house, and she did like her room, everyone was most kind, oh yes dear, it was the right thing, I should have done it years ago, I really am very settled. And Rosamund said that she was, too, said that it was fine, really, just as Addy told me, a lovely place, such kind people, and Alec had been and he agreed. All the same, I was worried, I wasn't sure. She had been so independent always, so energetic, so very much her own person all her life, I couldn't see her in a Home, however nice and however sensible a move it was – and she was eighty-six and had had two nasty falls the previous winter – I liked to think of her as she was when we were children, and went to stay at the house in Wales, striding over the hills with the dogs, rowing on the lake, getting up those colossal picnics for us all. I always loved her, she was such fun. I wish you had known her. And of course, I wish that one of us could have had her, but there really wasn't room to make her comfortable and, oh other feeble-sounding reasons which are real reasons, nonetheless. She had never asked me to visit her, that wasn't her way. Only the more she didn't ask, the more I knew that I should, the guiltier I felt. It was just such a terrible year, what with one thing and another. But now I was going. It had been a beautiful day for the drive too. I had stopped twice, once in a village, once in a small market town and explored churches and little shops, and eaten lunch and had a pot of tea and taken a walk along the banks of a river in the late sunshine, and the berries, I remember had been thick and heavy, clustered on the boughs. I'd seen a jay and two deer once, like magic, a kingfisher, flashing blue as blue across a hump-backed bridge. I'd had a sort of holiday really. But now I was tired, I would be glad to get there. It was very nice that they had a guest-room, and I didn't have to stay alone in some hotel. It meant I could really spend all my time with Aunt Addy. Besides, you know how I have always hated hotels, I lie awake thinking of the hundreds of people who've slept in the bed before me. Little Dornford 1^1/$_2$ m. But as I turned right and the road narrowed to a single track, between trees, I began to feel nervous, anxious, I prayed that it would be all right, that Aunt Addy had been telling the truth.

'You'll come to the church', they had said, and a row of three cottages, and then there is the sign to Farthing House, at the bottom of the drive. I had seen no other car since leaving the cathedral town seven miles back on the main road. It was very quiet, very out of the way. I wondered if Addy minded. She had always been alone up there in her own house but some-how now that she was so old and infirm, I thought she might have liked to be nearer some bustle, perhaps actually in a town. And what about the others, a lot of old women isolated out here together? I shivered sud-denly and peered forwards along the darkening lane. The church was just ahead, the car lights swept along a yew hedge, a lych gate, caught the shoulder of a gravestone. I slowed down. FARTHING HOUSE. It was a neat, elegantly lettered sign, not too prominent and at least it did not proclaim itself Residential Home. The last light was fading in the sky behind a copse of bare beech trees, the sun dropping down, a great red, frost-rimmed ball. I saw the drive, a wide lawn, the remains of a bonfire of leaves, smouldering by itself in a corner. Farthing House. I don't know exactly what my emotions had been up to that moment. I was very tired, with that slightly dazed, confused sensation that comes after a long drive and the attendant concentration. And I was apprehensive. I so wanted to be happy about Aunt Addy, to be sure that she was in the right place to spend the rest of her life – or maybe I just wanted to have my conscience cleared so I could bowl off home again in a couple of days with a blithe heart, untroubled guilt and be able to enjoy the coming Christmas. But as I stood on the black and white marbled floor of the entrance porch I felt something else and it made me hesitate before ringing the bell. What was it? Not fear or anxiety, no shudders. I am being very careful now, it would be too easy to claim that I had sensed something sinister, that I was shrouded at once in the atmosphere of a haunted house. But I did not, nothing of that sort crossed my mind. I was only overshadowed by a curious sadness – I don't know exactly how to describe it – a sense of loss, a melancholy. It descended like a damp veil about my head and shoulders. But it lifted, or almost, the cloud passed after a few moments. Well, I was tired, I was cold, it was the back end of the year, and perhaps I had caught a chill, which often manifests itself first as a sudden change of mood into a lower key.

The only other thing I noticed was the faintest smell of hospital antiseptic. That depressed me a bit more. Farthing House wasn't a hospital or even a nursing home proper and I didn't want it to seem so to Aunt Addy, not even in this slight respect. But in fact, once I was inside, I no longer noticed it at all, there was only the faintest smell of furniture polish, and fresh chrysanthemums and, somewhere in the background, a light, spicy smell of baking. The smells that greeted me were all of a piece with the rest of the welcome. Farthing House seemed like an individual private home. The antiques in the hall were good, substantial pieces and they had been well cared for over the years, there were framed photographs on a sideboard, flowers in jugs and bowls, there was an old, fraying, tapestry-covered armchair on which a fat cat slept beside a fire. It was quiet, too, there was no rattling of trolleys or buzzing of bells. And the matron did not call herself one. 'You are Mrs Flower – how nice to meet you.' She put out her hand. 'Janet Pearson.' She was younger than I had expected. Probably in her late forties. A small King Charles spaniel hovered about her waving a frond-like tail. I relaxed. I spent a good evening in Aunt Addy's company; she was so settled and serene and yet still so full of life. Farthing House was well run, warm and comfortable, and there was good, home-cooked dinner with fresh vegetables and an excellent lemon meringue pie. The rooms were spacious, the other residents pleasant but not over-obtrusive. Something else was not as I had expected. It had been necessary to reserve the guest-room and bathroom well in advance, but when Mrs Peterson took my bag and led me up the handsome staircase, she told me that after a serious leak in the roof had caused damage, it was being redecorated. 'So I've put you in Cedar – it happens to be free just now.' She barely hesitated as she spoke. 'And it's such a lovely room, I'm sure you'll like it.' How could I have failed? Cedar Room was one of the two largest in the house, on the first floor, with big bay windows over-looking the garden at the back – though now the deep red curtains had been drawn against the early evening darkness. 'Your Aunt is just across the landing.'

'So they've put you in Cedar,' Addy said later when we were having a drink in her own room. It wasn't so large, but I preferred it simply, I think, because there was so much familiar furniture, even the club fender we used to sit on to toast our toes as children. 'Yes. It seems a bit big for one person, but it's very handsome. I'm surprised it's vacant.' Addy winked at me. 'Well, of course it *wasn't...*' For an instant that feeling of unease and melancholy passed over me like a shadow again. 'Now buck up, don't look wan, there isn't time.' And she plunged me back into family chat and cheerful rec- ollections, interspersed with sharp observations about her fellow residents, so that I was almost entirely com- fortable again. I remained so until we parted at getting on for half past eleven. We had spent so much of the evening alone together, and then joined some of the others in one of the lounges, where an almost party- like atmosphere had developed, with banter and happy talk, which had all helped to revive my first impressions of Farthing House and Addy's place there. It was not until I closed the door of my room and was alone and was forced to acknowledge again what had been at the back of my mind all the time, almost like having a person at my shoulder, though just out of sight. I was in this large, high-ceilinged room because it was free, its previous occupant having recently died. I knew no more, and did not want to know, had firmly refrained from asking any questions. Why should it matter? It did not. As a matter of fact, it still does not, it had no bearing at all on what happened, but I must set it down because I feel I have to tell the whole truth and part of the truth is that I was unsettled, slightly nervous frame of mind as I got ready for bed, because of what I knew, and because I could not help wondering whether whoever had occupied Cedar Room had died in it, perhaps even in this bed. I was, as you might say, almost expecting to have bad dreams or to see a ghost. There is just one other thing. When we were all in the lounge, the talk had inevitably been of former homes and families, the past in general, and Addy had wanted some photographs from upstairs. I had slipped out to fetch them for her. It was very quiet in the hall. The doors were heavy and soundproof, though from behind one I could just hear some faint notes of recorded music, but the staff quarters were closed off and silent. So I was quite certain that I heard it, the sound was unmistakable. It was a baby crying. Not a cat, not a dog. They are quite different, you know. What I heard from some distant room on the ground floor was the cry of a newborn baby. I hesitated. Stopped. But it was over at once, and it did not come again. I waited, feeling uncertain. But then, from the room with the music, I heard the muffled signature of the ten o'clock news. I went on up the staircase. The noise had come from the television room then. Except, you see, that deep down and quite surely, I knew that it had not. I may have had odd frissons about my room but once I was actually in bed and settling down to read a few pages of *Sense and Sensibility* before going to sleep, I felt quite composed and cheerful. The only thing wrong was that the room still seemed far too big for one person. There was ample furniture and yet it was as though someone else ought to be there. I find it difficult to explain precisely. I was very tired. And Addy was happy, Farthing House was everything I had hoped it would be, I had had a most enjoyable evening, and the next day we were to go out and see something of the countryside and later, hear sung Evensong at the cathedral. I switched out the lamp. At first I thought it was as quiet outside the house as in, but after a few minutes, I heard the wind sifting through the bare branches and sighing towards the windows and away. I felt like a child again, snug in my little room under the eaves. I slept. I dreamed almost at once and with extraordinary vividness, and it was, at least to begin with, a most happy dream. I was in St Mary's, the night after you were born, lying in my bed in that blissful, glowing, untouchable state when the whole of the rest of life seems suspended and everything irrelevant but this. You were there in your crib beside me, though I did not look at you. I don't think anything happened in the dream and it did not last very long. I was simply there in the past and utterly content. I woke with a start, and as I came to, it was with that sound in my ears, the crying of the baby that I had heard as I crossed the hall earlier that evening. The room was quite dark. I knew at once where I was and yet I was still half within my dream – I remember that I felt a spurt of disappointment that it had *been* a dream and I was actually there, a new young mother again with you beside me in the crib. How strange, I thought, I wonder why. And then something else happened – or no, not 'happened'. There just *was* something else, that is the only way I can describe it.

I had the absolutely clear sense that someone else had been in my room – not the hospital room of my dream, but this room in Farthing House. No one was there now, but minutes before I woke, I knew that they had been. I remember thinking, someone is in the next bed. But of course, there was no bed, just mine. After a while I switched on the lamp. All was as it had been when I had gone to sleep. Only that sensation, that atmosphere was still there. If nothing else had happened at Farthing House, I suppose in time I would have decided I had half-dreamed, half-imagined it, and

forgotten. It was only because of what happened afterwards that I remembered so clearly and knew with
such certainty that my feeling had been correct. I got
up, went over to the tall windows and opened the curtains a little. There was a clear, star-pricked sky and a
thin paring of moon. The gardens and the dark countryside all around were peaceful and still. But I felt
oppressed again by the most profound melancholy of
spirit, the same terrible sadness and sense of loss that
had overcome me on my arrival. I stood there for a
long time, unable to release myself from it, before
going back to bed to read another chapter of Jane
Austen, but I could not concentrate properly and in
the end grew drowsy. I heard nothing, saw nothing,
and I did not dream again. The next morning my
mood had lightened. There had been a slight frost during the night, and the sun rose on a countryside dust-
ed over with rime. The sky was blue, trees set in dark
pencil strokes against it. We had a good day Aunt Addy
and I, enjoying one another's company, exploring
churches and antique shops, having a pub lunch, and
an old-fashioned muffin and fruitcake tea after the
cathedral service. It was as we were eating that I asked
suddenly, 'What do you know about Farthing House?'
Seeing Aunt Addy's puzzled look, I went on, 'I just
mean, how long has Mrs Pearson been there, who had
it before, all that sort of thing. Presumably it was once
a family house.' 'I have an idea someone told me it had
been a military convalescent home during the war.

Why do you ask?' I thought of Cedar Room the previous night, and that strange sensation. *What* had it been? Or who? But I found that I couldn't talk about it for some reason, it made me too uneasy. 'Oh, nothing. Just curious.' I avoided Addy's eye.

That evening, the matron invited me to her own room for sherry, and to ask if I was happy about my aunt. I reassured her, saying all the right, polite things. Then she said, 'And have you been quite comfortable?' 'Oh yes.' I looked straight at her. I thought she might have been giving me an opening – I wasn't sure. And I almost did tell her. But again, I couldn't speak of it. Besides, what was there to tell her? I had heard a baby crying – from the television. I'd had an unusual dream, and an odd, confused sensation when I woke from it that someone had just left my room. Nothing. 'I've been extremely comfortable,' I said firmly. 'I feel quite happy about everything.' Did she relax just visibly, smile a little too eagerly, was there a touch of relief in her voice when she next spoke? I don't know whether or not I dreamed that night. It seemed that one minute I was in a deep sleep, and the next that someone had woken me. As I came to, I know I heard the echo of crying in my ears, or in my inner ear, but a different sort of crying this time, not that of a baby, but a desperate, woman's sobbing. The antiseptic smell was faintly there again too, my awareness of it was mingled with that of the sounds. I sat bolt upright. The previous night, I had had the sensation of someone having just been in my room. Now, I saw her. There was another bed in the opposite corner of the room, close to the window, and she was getting out of it. The room felt horribly cold. I remember being conscious of the iciness on my hands and face. I was wide awake, I am quite sure of that, I could hear my own heart pounding, see the bedside table, and the lamp and the blue binding of *Sense and Sensibility* in the moonlight. I know I was not dreaming, so much so that I almost spoke to the woman, wondering as I saw her what on earth they were thinking of to put her and her bed in my room while I was asleep. She was young, with a flowing, embroidered night-gown, high necked and long sleeved. Her hair was long too, and as pale as her face. Her feet were bare. But I could not speak to her, my throat felt paralysed. I tried to swallow, but even that was difficult, the inside of my mouth was so dry.

She seemed to be crying. I suppose that was what I had heard. She moved across the room towards the door and has held her arms out as if she were begging someone to give her something. And that terrible melancholy came over me again, I felt inconsolable hopeless and sad. The door opened. I know that because a rush of air came in to the room, and it went even colder, but somehow I did not see her put her hand to the knob and turn it. All I know is that she had gone, and that I was desperate to follow her, because I felt that she needed me in some way. I did not switch on the lamp or put on my dressing-gown, I half ran to

catch her up. The landing outside was lit as if by a low
flickering candle flame. I saw the door of Aunt Addy's
room but the wood looked darker, and there were
some pictures on the walls that I had not noticed
before. It was still so cold my breath made little haws
of white in front of my face. The young woman had
gone. I went to the head of the staircase. Below, it was
pitch dark. I heard nothing, no footstep, no creak of
the floorboards. I was too frightened to go any further.
As I turned, I saw that the flickering light had faded
and the landing was in darkness too. I felt my way,
trembling, back to my own room and put my hand on
the doorknob. As I did so I heard from far below, in the
recesses of the house, the woman's sobbing and a calling – it might have been out of a name, but it was too
faint and far away for me to make it out. I managed to
stumble across the room and switch on the lamp. All
was normal. There was just one bed, my own. Nothing
had changed. I looked at the clock. It was a little after
three. I was soaked in sweat, shaking, terrified. I did
not sleep again that night but sat up in the chair
wrapped in the eiderdown with the lamp on, until the
late grey dawn came around the curtains. That I had
seen a young woman, that she had been getting out of
another bed in my room, I had no doubt at all. I had
not been dreaming, as I certainly had on the previous
night. The difference between the two experiences was
quite clear to me. She had been there. I had never
either believed or disbelieved in ghosts, scarcely ever

thought about the subject at all. Now, I knew that I had seen one. And I could not throw off not only my fear but the depression her presence inflicted on me. Her distress and agitation, whatever their cause, had affected me profoundly, and from the first moment of my arrival at the door of Farthing House. It was a dark, dreadful, hopeless feeling and with it there was also a sense of foreboding. I was due to leave the home the following morning but when I joined Aunt Addy for breakfast I felt wretched, tense and strained, quite unfit for a long drive. When I went to Mrs Pearson's office and explained simply that I had not slept well, she expressed concern at once and insisted that I stay on another night. I wanted to, but I did not want to remain in Cedar Room. When I mentioned it, very diffidently, Mrs Pearson gave me a close look and I waited for her to question me but she did not, only told me, slipping her pen nervously between her fingers that there simply was not another vacant room in the house. So I said that of course it did not matter, it was only that I had always felt uneasy sleeping in very large rooms, and laughed it off, trying to reassure her. She pretended that I had. That morning, Aunt Addy had an appointment with the visiting hairdresser. I didn't feel like sitting about reading papers and chatting in the lounge. They were nice women, the other residents, kind and friendly and welcoming but I was on edge and still enveloped in sadness and foreboding. I needed time to myself. The weather didn't help. It

had gone a degree or two warmer and the rise in temperature had brought a dripping fog and low cloud
that masked the lines of the countryside. I trudged
around Farthing House gardens but the grass was soaking wet and the sight of the dreary bushes and black
trees lowered my spirits further. I set off down the lane,
past three cottages. A dog barked from one, but the
others were silent and apparently empty. I suppose that
by then I had begun to wallow slightly in my mood
and I decided that I might as well go the whole hog
and visit the church and its overgrown little graveyard.
It was bitterly cold inside. There were some good brasses and a wonderful ornate eighteenth century monu-
ment to a pious local squire, with florid rhymes and
madly grieving angels. But the stained glass was in ugly
'uncut moquette' colours, as Stephen would have said,
and besides it was actually colder inside the church
than out. I had a prowl around the graveyard, looking
here and there at epitaphs. There were a couple of
minor gems but otherwise all was plain, names and
dates and dullness and I was about to leave when my
eye was caught by some gravestones at the far side near
to the field wall. They were set a little apart and neatly
arranged in two rows. I bent down and deciphered the
faded inscriptions. They were all the graves of babies,
newborn or a few days old, and dating from the early
years of the century. I wondered why so many, and
why all young babies. They had different surnames,
though one or two recurred. Had there been some

dreadful epidemic in the village? Had the village been
much larger then, if there had been so many young
families? At the far end of the row were three adult
sized stones. The inscriptions on two had been mossed
over but one was clear. Eliza Maria Dolly Died January
20 1902. Aged 19 years. And also her infant daughter.
As I walked thoughtfully back I saw an elderly man
dismount from a bicycle beside the gate and pause,
looking towards me. 'Good morning! Gerald
Manberry, vicar of the parish. Though really I am
semi-retired, there isn't a great deal for a full-time man
to take care of nowadays. I see you have been looking
at the poor little Farthing House graves.' 'Farthing
House?' 'Yes, just down the lane. It was a home for
young women and their illegitimate babies till the turn
of the century until the last war. Then a military convalescent home, I believe. It's a home for the elderly
now of course.' How bleak that sounded. I told him
that I had been staying there. 'But the graves...' I said.
'I suppose a greater number of babies died around the
times of birth then, especially in those circumstances.
And mothers too I fear. Poor girls. It's all much safer
now. A better world. A better world.' I watched him
wheel his ancient bicycle round to the vestry door,
before beginning to walk back down the empty lane
towards Farthing House. But I was not seeing my sur-
roundings or hearing the caw-cawing of the rooks in
the trees above my head. I was seeing the young
woman in the night-gown, her arms outstretched, and

hearing her cry and feeling again that terrible sadness and distress. I thought of the grave of Eliza Maria Dolly, 'and also her infant daughter.' I was not afraid any more, not now that I knew who she was and why she had been there, getting out of her bed in Cedar Room, to go in search of her baby. Poor, pale, distraught young thing, she could do no one harm.

I slept well that night, I saw nothing, heard nothing, although in the morning I knew, somehow, that she had been there again, there was the same emptiness in the room and the imprint of her sad spirit upon it. The fog cleared and it was a pleasant winter day, intermittently sunny. I left for home after breakfast, having arranged that Aunt Addy was to come to us for Christmas. She did so and we had a fine time, as happy as we all used to be together, with Stephen and I, Rosamund, Alec and the others. I shall always be glad of that, for it was Addy's last Christmas. She fell down the stairs at Farthing House the following March, broke her hip and died of a stroke a few days later. They took her to hospital and I saw her there, but afterwards, when her things were to be cleared up, I couldn't face it. Stephen and Alec did everything. I never went back to Farthing House. I often thought about it though, even dreamed about it. An experience like that affects you profoundly and for ever. But I could not have spoken about it, not to anyone at all. If ever a conversation touched upon ghosts I kept silent. I had seen one. I know. That was all.

*

Some years afterwards, I learned that Farthing House had closed to residents, been sold and then demolished, to make room for a new development – the nearby town was spreading out now. Little Dornford had become a suburb. I was sad. It had been, in most respects, such a good and happy place. Then, only a week ago, I saw the name again, quite by chance, it leaped at me from the newspaper. You may remember the case, though you would not have known of any personal connection. A young woman stole a baby, from its pram outside a shop. The child had only been left for a moment or two but apparently she had been following and keeping watch, waiting to take it. It was found eventually, safe and well. She had looked after it, so I suppose it could have been worse, but the distress caused to parents was obviously appalling. You can imagine that now, can't you? They didn't send her to prison, she was taken into medical care. Her defence was that she had stolen the child when she was out of her right mind after the death of her own baby, not long before. The child was two days old. Her address was given as Farthing House, Little Dornford. I think of it constantly, see the young, pale, distraught woman, her arms outstretched, searching, hear her sobbing, and the crying of the baby. But I imagine that she has gone, now that she has what she was looking for.

THE ALBATROSS

It was Wednesday. He had gone along the beach as usual for the fish. Nobody else bought fish that way, now, in small, individual pieces, straight from the men, nobody else. He always felt ashamed, trudging very slowly along the great sweep of shingle, the paper for it ready under his arm, he did not want to get there. He saw the men in their little dark huts lined up behind the boats, felt them looking out at him, laughing.

Though they were easy enough with him when he was there, they said nothing as they slit their long knives down the belly of a fish and gouged out the slippery pink innards, looking at the weight of the piece they had given him, guessing a price. And Duncan said nothing to them, had never done so, in all the time he had been coming down here, nothing at all, after he had asked for what he wanted. Only smelled the oil and brine and tar of the huts, and the thick tobacco from their pipes, only shifted his boots upon the wooden floor. He dared not wonder what they really thought of him, or how they talked, as he went away, back towards Tide Street, his heart still thumping inside him with relief after dread.

At Todd's fish shop in Market Cross, it was different, there were the grained, stained boxes piled up against the wall, from Grimsby and Yarmouth and Hull, there were kippers ~~and~~ mackerel and turbot and pink-spotted plaice, upon the slab.

'You don't go buying any of our fish, from that Todd's, thank you, you go down the beach like I tell you, that's what we've always done, isn't it? I'm not paying good money in aid of Todd's gold-painted signs and fancy new refrigerators.' For once, years ago, he was pushing her wheelchair down Market Cross, and there had been a great blue lorry and seven men heaving a new refrigerator into Todd's shop. Later on came the newly-painted sign, swinging in the East wind. She had never forgotten.

So that he must still go, every Wednesday morning, or else in the late afternoon, when he returned from the Big House, down to buy just enough for the two of them, from the fishermen on the beach. It was always Wednesday.

'Not cod,' she had told him, over and over again, and written it down with one of the thick, black carpenter's pencils she kept all about the cottage. She underlined the words twice, as he waited.

'NOT COD.'

'There's only cod, boy,' the man said, Davey Ward this

time, the only one of them in the huts, Davey Ward with the scarlet burn down one side of his face, making the skin shine. He had turned and slung the fish guts into the bucket with the rest, rolling the cod up briskly into Duncan's paper. 'Nothing much but cod, this time of season.'

Duncan stood dumbly, alarmed by the huge size of the man, in the tiny hut. He did not know whether one man, looming over him, were as bad, or worse, than all of them together, talking.

Davey Ward delved his thick fingers about in the pockets of his trousers, feeling for change.

Outside it was all but dark, the January sky like slate, and moving with clouds. The beacon flashed green, on-off, on-off, out to sea beyond the breakwater. Duncan walked down nearer to the waterline and then away, face into the wind, listening to the crunch and chop of his rubber boots as they bit into the shingle.

Behind him, Davey Ward raised the bucket and tossed the fish offal into the sea, and the gulls lifted at once off pebbles and water and came down from all the red rooftops of Heype, gathering overhead, rawking for their food.

'What did I say about it? Just this morning? What did I say?'

Duncan stood helplessly in front of her wheelchair, holding the open parcel in his outstretched hands,

looking down at where the cold, flat strips of fish lay,
marble-white.

'What did I say?'

And written down, too, as she wrote everything
down for him, every message, every demand, every list.
Years before he could read himself, the notes had been
there, to be handed to other people. He had not read
anything until he was ten.

'NOT COD' she had written, and folded the torn-
off piece of greaseproof paper into a square and held
him to her by the edge of his coat, while she stuffed it
into the left-hand pocket.

'Look now, I'm putting it in here, in your pocket on
this side, don't you forget where it is when you get
there, just you think on.'

He did not need the pieces of paper, the written
messages and lists, he had never needed them, he could
remember. So that always, when he got out of sight of
the cottage, he took them out and tore them up into
small pieces and threw them away. For all these years,
he had done so, because the notes shamed him, they
were things he hated. She used her hands to write
them, and so, to carry them in his pocket would have
meant that he must carry *her* with him, even when he
was away from the house. He would not do that, he
did not need the lists. But he no longer tried to make
her understand, or believe him.

'You'll have it written down,' she said propelling her
wheelchair viciously in and out of doorways, all about

the small kitchen. 'You don't remember things, you never have, not properly, you need it written down. I'm your mother aren't I, do you think I don't know about it better than you?'

And she was not the only one. Mrs Reddingham-Lee wrote things down for him, if there were more than two jobs she wanted him to do, or any message to be taken, things to be fetched. He worked for Mrs Reddingham-Lee, at the Big House.

'Now Duncan, come here – now, here is your list, I have written it all down, there is nothing for you to do but give it to them, nothing for you to worry about.'

She spoke to him in a very clear tone of voice, a little more loudly than she would speak to any other.

'Duncan is perfectly all right,' she told her friends, 'he is perfectly reliable, Duncan is not a defective. He is just a little slow, he has not always got everything quite clear in his mind.'

She felt, though she would not have said so, that the world owed a little thanks to her, some special grace or other, because she employed the boy Duncan.

But it was not the same with Cragg. Cragg had known him since he was born, eighteen years, and known his mother – Cragg and Mrs Cragg. Though they had nothing to do with them, they were not friends. But alone with the boy, working during the day in the stables and toolsheds, the cellars and the garden and the conservatories of the Big House, Cragg did not give out any written lists, he wasted no breath on repetition. Cragg gave him orders, one, two, three, harsh as bullets. Duncan heard them and remembered, there were no mistakes.

He did not know which way he preferred to be treated – for there had only ever been that simple choice: between the written-down messages and careful speaking of Mrs Reddingham-Lee, and the orders of Cragg. It was one or the other of these ways with everyone who knew him in Heype. And then there was his mother.

'What did I say?'

He wanted to put the fish down, he could smell the sharp, briny smell, filling the back kitchen, and his hands were cold and numb from it, underneath.

'Not cod, I said it twice, more than twice, I wrote it down, didn't I? Didn't I write it down?'

'It's all there was.'

He wanted to ask her what else he should have done, whether she would have wanted him to come back with nothing at all, what they would have eaten for supper then, and how could he have asked for the fish and then rejected it when he saw that it was cod, when it had all been done so quickly, taken and slit open, filleted and wrapped by Davey Ward. But he said nothing.

'I hate it, cod. I hate the sight of it, all filled up with water, I told you that.'

'It's all they catch just now, it's all there is. In January. It's the bad season.'

'The bad season,' she echoed his tone of voice. 'What do you know about that?'

'He told me. He said. There is nothing else, only the cod.'

'That's all they want to tell you. You don't know anything about it. Your Mrs Reddingham-Lee doesn't have cod, cod, cod, up at the Big House. No.'

'They get their fish at Todd's.'

'Well you don't, you go along the beach, always have done. I'm not buying from that Todd.'

Hilda Pike's fingers still rubbed up and down the rims of the wheels, he heard her voice saying what it always said to him, over and over again, like the waves turning themselves on to the beach.

'You never listen, that's your trouble, isn't it? You dream. It's no wonder you're like you are, you never try to help yourself, never.'

Sometimes, when she began like this, and at other times too, for no reason, he felt a confused anger welling up inside himself, so that, as a small boy, he had gone along through the marshes, beside the river, for hours, beating and beating at the reeds with a stick, or throwing pebbles one after another, hard into the sea. Once, he had kicked his own feet against the school wall until the canvas of his plimsolls split, and his toes were grazed and bruised and bleeding.

Not now, not for a long time. Now, he listened and felt numb. Yet he was more vulnerable, too, as he grew up, even less able to defend himself. But now, he did nothing, only looked after her, pushing the wheelchair up and down the streets, lifting and carrying her, helping her to dress, only learned to cook and clean and do the work they gave him up at the Big House. Only went and stood for hours on end, looking at the sea.

The kitchen had gone quite dark, he could just see his mother's hands, white on the chair wheels, and the steel of her spectacle frames, the metal of a saucepan on the black stove. 'Who was it sold you that?'

'He was the only one there, Davey Ward, he said…'

'Mr Ward.'

'Yes, Mr Ward.'

'He's nothing to do with you, he isn't a friend, none of them are. Calling him by his name! They've nothing to do with us at all.'

'No.'

But Duncan thought suddenly of Ted Flint and his mind filled with pictures, like the tide tumbling into a rock pool. Ted Flint was his own age, Ted Flint, with the dense blue whorls and stripes of tattoo covering his arms and chest, his own boat.

'You go for the fish and you come away again. That's all. They're not the sort of people you want to get in with, haven't I always told you that? Didn't I tell you from the start, from when you were at school?'

'Yes,' he said. 'Yes.'

'We live our own life, we keep ourselves to ourselves, in this town.'

He had wondered, ever since he could remember,

why she had come here with him, when he was one month old, why she had settled in this place at all. He knew almost nothing about her, she would not tell him of the past. 'We keep ourselves to ourselves in this town.'

But he had always lived here, he had gone to school and then left it, and looked after her since the accident, he did not know any other place. He had walked the streets and the paths inland along the river bank beside the flat, still marshes, he had known winter and summer, autumn and spring here, in Heype and nowhere else, he knew every line and fold in the faces of the people, every brick of the cottages opposite their own in Tide Street. He belonged here, even if, lately, he had begun wanting to go away. Yet she talked as if they would not stay here, as if he must not attach himself to anything or anyone. She had chosen to come, chosen it as their place, but for eighteen years, they had lived quite apart from it. Because of the accident, she could never move elsewhere, she was bound to the town and the cottage and to her wheelchair. Nothing was said. Walking along the sea wall, past the old quay and the martello tower, and then on for miles across the pale stretches of shingle, Duncan thought, she will not let me go, or truly stay, I can neither have this nor that, nothing I want. But he could not sort it out, he had never understood the workings of his mother's mind, nor questioned any of her reasons.

'Well?' she said now, and spun round suddenly in

the chair, so that he started backwards, coming up against the edge of the wooden draining board, beside the sink. She had unhooked her stick and reached up with it to switch on the light.

'You'd better cook it, hadn't you? Fry it, cod or whatever it is, there's nothing else to eat.'

'No. I asked. I did ask but he said there wasn't anything else. Only the cod!' He was trembling a little, with the effort of trying to explain to her.

His mother looked at him out of the sharp, tight-skinned face, and he saw a momentary softening cross it, like a shadow on the surface of the sea. But it was nothing more than scorn. 'You'd believe anything,' she said, 'do anything they asked you. You've always been like that. Soft. They could tell you anything at all.'

He wanted to cry, holding the cold fish, because he had not done right, because he was as he was and could not please her.

But, all that day, there had been the thought of going away, filling his mind. On his own, of going wherever he chose.

It was after Cragg had told him about Southampton. Usually, Cragg told him nothing, did not talk at all, except to give out orders, even if they were doing some job together. Not even over their lunch. In good weather, they sat outside, on the green bench behind the conservatory, where the sun caught their faces, reflected off the glass. The Big House was built on the last of the cliff ledges up above the town,

it overlooked all the other roof-tops of Heype, as they
went down in layers to the sea. But in winter, there was
a coke brazier in the toolshed and they sat on upturned
boxes and a broken wicker chair, eating their sandwiches, drinking tea from flasks.

Long ago, Mrs Reddingham-Lee had said, 'There is
the kitchen, Mr Cragg, goodness me! You have no need
to sit in that dark old shed, you should come and be
comfortable in the kitchen.' And she had offered the
services of the daily woman, Mrs Beale, for freshly
brewed pots of tea.

Three years ago, when Duncan had come to work
here, she had offered yet again. Cragg had said no. 'No,
thank you very much,' for he was a stubborn man,
independent, he wanted to eat his sandwiches out
of the way of the house and of Mrs Reddingham-
Lee. In the shed, he was his own master. He drank
from the private flask of tea put up by his wife each
morning.

Duncan cut his own sandwiches, prepared his own
flask, he had not dared to go against the orders of
Cragg, though he would have liked to sit in the warm
kitchen, to feel a sense of belonging inside the Big
House. They sat and drank and ate for forty-five minutes, summer and winter, between twelve-fifteen and
one. It was hot in the toolshed, the brazier glowed red,
piled up with coke. Cragg unlaced his boots and loosened them and then read his newspaper from cover to
cover, hunched up against the wall, saying nothing. He

was a man with a rough-textured, bumpy face, a secret expression.

But today, Duncan had mended the broken hammock. He had sat just outside the toolshed and knotted patiently in and out with a ball of thick twine, until it had been complete. Cragg had slung and tied it between the two apple trees and climbed up to test the strength. Out of the house, down through the drawing-room windows and across the lawn, came Mrs Reddingham-Lee. 'The hammock! Oh, now, Duncan, you *are* clever, how very clever of you! You have mended the hammock, and just when I was so sure we must have a new one, it looked so badly torn and eaten away. How splendid!' and she clapped her hands together and gave the hammock, with Cragg in it, a little push.

'That'll hold,' Cragg said. 'Yes,' and nodded, climbing out and down. He had doubted if the boy would manage it, in spite of his slow patience, so that now, grudgingly, he was pleased, he liked to think of things saved and mended, of a job satisfactorily done.

Which was why he allowed himself to talk, briefly, over their lunch in the toolshed, about a visit to his daughter, married to a docker in Southampton.

'*You've* never seen anything like it, I'll tell you, you never have. The ships. Big as Heype church, easy. Yes, I wouldn't doubt it.'

Duncan dared not move, scarcely dared breathe, sitting in the dry, soil-smelling shed, for fear that Cragg might notice his presence and stop talking, go back to his newspaper and deny him any further glimpses into this new, miraculous world.

'You've got the liners, of course, those to America and South Africa and such. Ships you see there, they've been across all the seas of the world.'

Duncan tried to picture them and failed, he had only a dim vision of something as big as a church and of the sea stretching away for thousands of pale blue miles. He thought, I could go. That's the thing I want to do. I could go. His head was filled with this picture, of the endless sea, and of his own sailing on it, far away.

'Great cranes they have, you see, swinging across with the cargoes, and the luggage. And all the people, rolling up in their smart cars, of course. The passengers.' Cragg bit hard into his slab of meat sandwich.

Anxious to show that he had something to contribute to a conversation between them, Duncan said, 'I saw the trawlers. At Lowestoft. I've been and seen those.' He was stammering.

'Lowestoft!'

Duncan shrank back into himself.

'I'm talking about ships, aren't I? Real ships. You've never seen anything like it.'

A gust of wind blew the door of the toolshed open suddenly, and there was the winter sky, bleached and grey as a gull's back. Cragg stood up.

'You want to take yourself off, get on a train, you

want to go and see them for yourself.' For he had not such a low opinion of Duncan's capabilities as others in Heype.

'Southampton?'

'Southampton docks, Portsmouth, anywhere. You've never have seen anything like it. They have day trips, down from London.'

Duncan screwed the plastic cup back on to the top of his flask and could not make it fit, his hands were trembling. I could go, he thought, I could go anywhere. Even though he had been no further than the port of Lowestoft, outside Heype. I could go.

'I want that bottom bed dug over,' Cragg said. 'Get out the big fork.'

Every now and again, throughout that day, the recollection of it had come back to him, and his heart began to pound with the shock, the impossibility and the excitement of it. It took him a long time, stabbing the big fork into the frost-hardened earth and turning it over, to sort out each separate part of the idea to get it clear in his head. The soil crumbled, sweet-smelling, and he bent down from time to time to pull out woody bits of old root, and fleshly white bulbs, from between the prongs of the fork. It was very cold. Behind him, the wind blew up the hill off the sea. When he rested for a moment, turning round, he could see it there, spreading flatly away, and the river, steel-coloured on the other side, running between the marshes. He would have been happy to work in the garden all the time. A yard away, a thrush pecked into the freshly-turned soil.

Ipswich. Yes. He would get on a bus at the end of Market Street and he would ride on that to Ipswich. It was a fair way, over twenty miles. He had never been. From Ipswich, the trains ran to London, and from London the trains ran everywhere, to any of the places he might choose. Though these were only names in his mind, he could not picture them, nor how he would get about in them, what he would do. He wished, after all, that there were another way, that he could walk down to the beach and get into a boat and go, as the fishermen all went, disappearing over the horizon. Though he knew that, in fact, none of them went far, only four or five miles out, to the sandbank. He had watched them for years, heard them talking about it and then tried to imagine how it would be, putting the boats out, nose facing the open sea. He had never been, never been on the water.

'The sea's not safe,' his mother said. 'You wouldn't do on the sea, you wouldn't know how to manage, you don't go off in any of those boats. That's a dangerous place.'

Then why had they come here, to a cottage in Tide Street? Though perhaps it was because she mistrusted the sea that they did not overlook it. Here, it was small and dark, sheltered behind the tall houses of the seafront.

'You keep away, it isn't any place for you, you leave

it alone.' As though the sea were some dangerous dog which he must never stroke. But she had been born beside it, he knew that much, in another town, farther up the coast. She had always lived there.

'Nobody could trust you in any boat, muddling about. You stay as you are.'

And now, he longed for the sea, watched it and walked beside it, and thought of how it would be, to get away, like the men, in the early morning. He remembered Cragg talking about the liners as big as churches, crossing all the seas of the world. All that. And yet he dared not go too near, when the water ran high and rough in winter, the surf bursting on the shingle in thunder and clouds of spray, he came away from it in dread.

The wind was dropping now, he felt the sweat run down his back, beneath the heavy jumper. There was a long, even line of darker soil, where he had worked his way right across the flower bed. He liked digging, he could do it well, and carefully, there was nothing about it to confuse him. The thrush hopped nearer, on its twig-like legs, and then froze, sensing his own stillness, waiting.

From the house, the voice of Mrs Reddingham-Lee. 'Duncan! Now come up here, Duncan, will you, there is something I would like you to get for me, in the village.'

At once, he began to be anxious about whether to leave the fork stuck here in the ground, whether he would have time to come back and finish the patch later, or if he ought to take it away now, into the shed, and clean it. Whichever he did, Cragg might tell him that he had been wrong. The day was no longer simple. His shirt stuck to his back, across the thin shoulders.

'Duncan!'

The thrush took off and flew across the garden, into a hedge. In the kitchen of the Big House, Mrs Reddingham-Lee sat down and wrote out a list on a fresh sheet of paper, in large capital letters.

I could go, Duncan thought. It's what Cragg said. *I could go.*

'That wall,' said Hilda Pike, 'that front wall, it's crumbling down, it's falling to pieces, the plaster's just coming away.'

She owned the cottage, she had come to Heype with £900, eighteen years ago, and bought and furnished it, and now it was falling apart, the builders were needed, painters and electricians and plumbers. But there was no longer any money.

'It looks bad,' she said, 'right on the street. It's a disgrace. That's not how decent people live.' For the cottage had always looked neat and tight and well-kept, for the eyes of neighbours, the two small windows up and down carefully curtained, the brick whitewashed and clean. There was a bit of path and a bit of garden and then the gate, and the wall which was coming down. None of the other cottages in Tide Street had any garden, people walked out of their front doors, straight into the road. Theirs was better, Hilda Pike said, theirs was different, though inside it was still poky and cramped, two up two down, and without much light. Down narrow alleys, running in between the houses that faced it, glimpses of the sea.

'You'll have to set it up again. You can get cement, and use what brick there is, you'll have to spend a Saturday and Sunday on that wall, it's a sight.'

They had eaten the fish supper, the cod she had not wanted, and he had done the washing up, while his mother dried, sitting close up beside him at the little sink, in her wheelchair.

In the front room, there was a log on the fire. Mrs Reddingham-Lee had sent him home from the Big House with a pile of logs, from the cut-down pear trees, a week before Christmas. Duncan had been terrified, pushing the wheelbarrow down the sloping lanes, for his mother would refuse them, as she refused all the gifts, and offers of help from others, from the neighbours, or people like Mrs Reddingham-Lee. He had worried about what he might do with the logs, where else they would go.

But she had not refused. '*They've* no use for old trees,' she had said, unaccountably, 'they can afford to throw them out, can't they? It's nothing to them, it's only wood. Wood's free.'

He had spent every morning for a week, sawing

them up into smaller pieces and then piled them most
carefully together, in a single pyramid, outside the back
door. He liked to look at them there, he would go and
lift one and feel the roughness and the weight between
his hands. It upset him, to watch them disintegrate
upon the fire.

Every piece of furniture had been in the cottage
since the beginning, she had come to Heype with
nothing and bought all of it, and no more since, so that
he knew the shape and colour and texture of everything, hated it all. Southampton, he thought, ships as
big as churches across all the seas of the world! I could
go anywhere, do anything. *I could go.* His head sang.

Ted Flint had gone, as soon as he left school, he had
gone on the trawlers from Lowestoft, sailing all winter
up to Denmark and Iceland, three, four months away
at a time. While he was gone, Duncan had thought
about him, tried to imagine what jobs he did, what the
ship smelled like, the look of the iced-up sea. He had
started his own job, at the Big House, what bits and
pieces Cragg would trust him with at first-picking up
old flower pots and washing the cars. In the streets of
Heype, he had seen Ted Flint's mother and wanted to
ask her questions, to know about the trawlers. But he
dared not. He had been at school with Ted Flint.

When he came back from the trawlers, he was huge,
taller than Davey Ward and coarse-bearded, his arms
covered with the blue tattoos. He had bought his own
boat, then, and set up, and the others had accepted

him at once, because he was a Heype man, he had gone away but still belonged. He was tough now, and often hot-tempered, he would take his boat out in the worst of the gales and seas, when the rest of them did not dare, they stayed behind to watch him and wait, talking about him in the wooden huts. Ted Flint. He was the same age as Duncan, rising nineteen. His father, and his father's father, had both gone down with the Heype lifeboat, a year after he was born. Ted Flint.

Duncan had thought, why did he come back here, why? He had seen him on the beach, hauling the boat in over the wooden struts, his hands like raw meat from the cold wind and water. Why? He had gone away and then come back, both of his own choice. Duncan could not understand any of it.

His mother sat with her chair drawn up close to the fire, and her fingers flicked so fast, in and out of the crochet, his eyes could never keep up with them. The white squares and circles of finished work were piling up beside her, on the tall stool. Even since the accident, she had done nothing else, evening after evening, except the crochet, here, or else sitting out in the tiny back yard, when it was summer In the Cottage Crafts shop, and Stevens the Draper's, and other shops in towns outside Heype, cushions and shawls and bedcovers made up from all the individual crocheted squares and circles, were expensively for sale. Duncan took the work and brought back the money, sealed in an envelope which he was not allowed to open, and sometimes, he took parcels, the crochet went as far as London, even. He thought about the distance it travelled, from his mother's flicking hands in Tide Street, until it reached the tables and beds and sofas of women like Mrs Reddingham-Lee.

'It's all work for no money,' Hilda Pike said, 'it's easy enough for them, getting it in, buying and selling, they've not the work, the hours and hours spent. I wouldn't choose to do it.'

Once, he had said in tears of misery and desperation, at the sight of the endlessly working fingers, 'Don't do it. You don't need to do it. There's what I get, I get money.'

He had never forgotten her face, open and bland with scorn, and pity, too, for this boy she had conceived and born and bred and who was too simple to help himself, or to be trusted, who could not be made to understand.

'*Your* money!'

He knew that she was right, even though they lived plainly enough, that what he brought home from the Big House, and the pension she got because of her accident, was nothing, nothing at all, that the fingers had to go on, flick-flick-flick, in and out of the endless crochet, if they were to live.

Why did we come here? What are we doing here? Where did it all begin? But she would not tell, would not speak to him about his father, or even about her own, about anything to do with the past. Except that, once a year, she had taken him – and now he took her – up the hill to the church, and there, she made him kneel down and pray to God for the eternal rest of his grandmother, who had died on that day. They took a single bunch of flowers, daffodils or anemones, and laid them on some ledge or step inside the church. That was all. She told him nothing about that woman who had been her mother, and so he had no picture in his mind upon which he could focus, it seemed an impossible thing, to pray about, a name, a ghost, a shadow. It was March, and the church was always cold. They stayed four or five minutes, only, in silence, and then came home.

Why did we come here?

'Don't you forget. You can do something about it on Saturday, that wall. That'll fall down altogether, otherwise.'

The pear log spluttered and then went dead again. They had only one lamp in the front room, up on the table behind her crochet. Everything seemed suddenly dark to him, all the furniture, the dresser and the shiny brown sofa, the stool and the grate and the oak-framed picture of a lake and two mountains. He was stifled, wanting to put out his hands and beat it all away.

'Where are you going? What's all that? Here – what do you think you're off to do, this time of night, Duncan Pike? What....'

But he had gone, banging the door and running

away from Tide Street, from the cottage and his mother and the broken-down wall.

Outside, it was calm. All afternoon, the wind had been dropping. Now, the sky was clear.

He ran hard for a long way, down Wash Alley and past the coastguard station, out on to the sea defence wall, until he had to stop and catch his breath. The blood was surging in his chest.

It was low water. The sea was flat and scarcely moving. There was a thin moon.

He began to walk, away from the town, on and on, towards the martello tower, looming up through the darkness. The air was raw on his face, beginning to freeze. He had not stopped to put on a jacket or boots, the soles of his shoes made scarcely any noise on the flat concrete slabs of the wall. He would not have walked on the beach, not at night, the crunching of his steps in the shingle would have deadened his hearing of the other night sounds, and he must always be listening, ready for what might come. Since he was a boy, he had grown used to all the sounds of the sea, and to those coming off the river and the marshes, he missed nothing.

He was beyond thinking now, only walked steadily on through the darkness. But feelings gathered inside him, like matter in a wound, and began to press outwards, until he wondered what he might do. He remembered his mother's fingers, working the endless crochet, and the dark little room, the splutter and smell of pear logs on the fire, her voice in his ears.

'*You* don't know. You can't do that. You're not to be trusted with anything. You'd never manage. What have you been able to do?'

And so they all spoke to him, too loudly, as though he were a deaf and dumb boy, they wrote things down for him in lists.

'*You* don't know.'

Again, he thought, I can go away, there is nothing I couldn't do. Ted Flint went away. *I could go.*

He stopped, and poked out to where the North Sea lay, stirring beyond him in the darkness. He could go anywhere, by himself.

But he knew why they did not trust him. He was slow, unable to sort things out into clear patterns, to make his way unaided through the maze of decisions and voices and small needs of every day, unable to explain. He was dependent on his mother, as she was upon him.

At school they had let him draw things, he had held his pencil in a tightly closed fist and never lifted it from the paper, so that all the lines were joined. He drew animals and ships and strangely shaped birds and decorated circles, round and round and round, he was happy doing so, thinking of nothing.

I could go.

The sound of the sea came to him, as it turned over and over on the pebbles, like the wind hissing through summer elm trees. But when he climbed off the wall and slid down the grass bang on to the path beside the river, the swish of the waves receded. Here, it was almost completely still. The water lapped a little up against the mud, and moved secretly in and out between reeds and rushes.

The moon sent long shadows off the martello tower, across the surface of the river. Duncan went closer, his shoes sinking into the rust-tinted mud, so that they made a small suck and hiss. He liked the slippery feel of it through the soles of them, the coldness. Out ahead, in hiding places all over the marshes, the birds would be, dead-still, half-sleeping, the curlews and thin-legged herons and the wild duck.

When he was much younger, they had tried to frighten him with stories about this place at night, about what happened on the river and in the marshes. Smugglers had come up here and been murdered hundreds of years ago and now their ghosts rose up and followed people, phospher gleamed on the water and false lights and voices led boatmen on to their deaths in the sucking bogs.

He had always been afraid of so many real, definite things, of other people and what they might do, and of the thoughts and feelings within himself. But he was not afraid of these tales that they told him in dark corners, behind the walls of the school, or when they followed him home down the town steps and into the alleys that led towards Tide Street. He could walk out here alone at night and never be afraid. It was different with people, for he could not defend himself against them, there seemed to him no way of predicting what they would do, he dreaded the sight of them, coming towards him, singly or together, their movements and booming voices and the way they might be going to treat him. He could only measure them very slowly, one at a time. Like Cragg. He knew Cragg a little, now, he was not so often startled by the things he said and did. But there were very few others. With the fishermen on the beach, he could never feel safe.

After a long time of standing, listening to the faint sounds, he came away again from the river, up the bank and back on to the wall. The tide was just turning. Looking back, he could see the lights of Heype, glittering up the hill. Then he walked on, he was around the other side of the tower and the emptiness and darkness of the beach and the marshes dropping down. Overhead there was a faint whistling, and then the beating of wings, two or three ducks, flying in from the sea.

He moved again, softly, through the pebbly soil and the sea grass, and into the dry moat running all the way round the tower. The stone walls were huge above him. Everything went dead still, the sound of both sea and river entirely blocked off inside the moat. There was a slab of broken concrete, overturned when they had been making the defence wall. Duncan sat down. He liked the tower. Nobody else seemed to come here now, he could settle behind it and never be seen, he felt protected.

Once, they had kept watch from here, looked out across the sea for the sight of some invading enemy. It was like the keep of a huge castle, the walls of the tower were thick as a man's arm, slabbed and brown-grey. Now, the look-out turret was half broken away, spaces in the stone were thick with climbing bindweed. There was a door at the bottom, you could climb up and get inside. Now, it swung away from its hinges, and beyond that, it was black. He had never gone in there. The others had. When he was at school, he had come and stood on the beach by himself and watched them, they had raced and leaped along the sea wall, and then gone swarming in, exploring cellars and all the rooms up the spiral staircase, until they reached the top and peered out of the turret. It was a dangerous place, crumbling down, private, forbidden. Everyone else had been into it. But he had never gone anywhere with any of them. They had pointed down at him, far below, and called out, waved their hands and shrieked with laughter, their voices carrying on the wind towards him and beyond, echoing far out to sea.

But none of them would dare to come here at night, not even now. When the tides ran high, the water flooded the cellars of the martello. At the beginning they had been used as dungeons, people said, men had been locked in there and left to drown.

The moon shone directly through the open door at

the top of the steps, so that he could see more than blackness, he could see a couple of steps, and then shadows a little way inside. Down here, it was quite sheltered, only his face was still cold, though a white frost was beginning to glisten thinly in between the grasses. All around him, there were bits of rock, and stone, twisted bolts of iron and old glass shaped smoothly into pebbles. He thought of what things he might find, hidden in the moat.

Once, walking on the beach near to the lifeboat, he had found a coin, coppery-looking and with some strange markings on it. The edges were quite smooth. He had been anxious about what to do with it, and in the end, had given it to one of the fishermen. The man had half-turned from mending his sprat nets, and slipped the coin in his pocket, nodding to Duncan, saying nothing.

His mother had screamed at him in fury, she made him return to the beach, told him that he must ask for the coin back. But he had not dared. He had walked to and fro endlessly in front of the boats, watching the man continue with his work on the nets, and seen the other men, too, he had heard them laughing and turned his face towards the sea. But he could not have gone near to the man with the coin again.

'I don't know,' he said, 'I didn't see him. I don't know which man he was.'

Her eyes had glittered with disbelief.

'That coin, that might be worth a hundred pounds,

more, that might have been anything. You! You can't be expected to know, you don't do any good for anybody. You find something on the beach next time and you bring it home here with you, don't you? Here to me. You remember.'

But he had never found anything again. Only the curiously shaped pebbles and bits of dry, hollowed-out driftwood, which he took home because he liked them and which his mother threw away. What she must have was the cottage tidy, carefully polished, orderly, the clearance of all bits and pieces.

Now, because he remembered how he had run out of the house so abruptly, giving no reason, thinking nothing of her, he felt a surge of pride and delight, he felt powerful, as though he were suddenly a man like Ted Flint, he could do anything. Though he did not forget the sound of her voice, calling him back, rising higher in anger and fear. For she was afraid to be left alone at night now, she kept her stick hooked over the back of the chair. Without him there, she was helpless, except to propel herself about between front room and kitchen. Besides, she did not trust him, nor believe that he was safe to be out on his own alone.

Something scuttled ahead of him along the tower, and then up the bank, through the sand and grasses. The tower was full of small animals, mice and rats and all the nesting birds. He liked them, any of them, he tried to find live things to hold between his hands.

Above his head, the stars were thick as apple blossom. He began to feel the cold, right through his body.

When he got up, he walked softly around the moat, past the gaping door and returned, to stand on the wall. The air was cold as steel coming off the sea.

'Duncan Pike!' The voice was no more than a whisper, below him on the dark beach.

'Duncan Pike!'

He neither moved nor spoke, he did nothing except wait. His limbs and all the nerves and muscles through his body felt loose and slack, his mind was brimming full, but stopped in its course like the river, overtaken by frost and ice. This was how it was with him, in fear, this or else violent confusion, which sent him pelting away. No single thought or feeling could be separated from the whole, coagulated mass.

'Duncan Pike!'

There was a scrabbling noise, a trundling and dragging of the shingle, and then the clang of metal, a bump, bump, bump, and someone breathing hard, straining with effort.

Two or three yards away from him, a figure emerged up the broad steps in the sea wall, pulling something up behind it. On the shoreline, a wave broke, creaming over softly and then rasping up the sand and pebbles. Silence. The figure began to back a little, closer to him, along the wall. He had not moved but now he knew who it was and his mind loosened a little, enough for him to recognise that he need not be afraid.

She reached his side and stopped. His shoulders were hunched up into his neck, in a defensive gesture, he was thin and slight as a twelve-year-old, in the dark sweater.

'Well now!

He could feel her looking at him closely, her small eyes searching him up and down. Old Beattie. He had not seen her for a week or two. Out on the sandbanks, the emerald flash-flashed, and then was dark again.

She was friendly towards him, he thought that was now certain. Though very few people in the town trusted her and she lived, Hilda Pike said, like a vulture, off the droppings of others. Every morning and evening she went along the beach, close to the shore, walking for miles, pushing the old pram, her head bent, eyes searching the ground. From time to time she parked the pram, and went to crouch, or even to kneel down, raking her fingers about through the pebbles and taking up this or that to throw into it.

There were always stories going about that she knew where to find amber, great lumps of it, somewhere out beyond Thereford Point, that Old Beattie was rich, going off with the stones to Ipswich and bringing back wads of notes to line the mattress of her bed. Others laughed, and said that she found rubbish, nothing, old plimsolls lost by children in the summer sea, and tin cans and wood for kindling. And if she was lucky, a penny or a sixpence. She was poor, they said, Beattie Thorpe had nothing but a pension. But nobody knew, not for certain, she was spied upon and guessed about and never completely trusted.

'Duncan Pike.'

'Yes,' he said in the end, stammering partly from the cold. And then, 'It's weeks. It's a long time. I've not seen you.'

She was still looking at him sideways on. What she wore was always the same, the old, bruise-coloured raincoat, long to her ankles, and seeming to billow out curiously, to be padded in odd places.

'Newspaper,' she had told him once, 'you tie it round yourself, underneath a woollen. Keeps out all the cold, that does.'

In the pram there were always newspapers, piled neatly, she collected them every so often from the back doors of houses. She went along the beach, and through the streets of Heype, untroubled by the worst of the weather, in gale and rain and sleet, her head was always uncovered. She wore the same pair of rubber boots, short and very wide at the tops, and faded by salt and sea to a faint coral pink.

Duncan turned his head to look at her, and she seemed to have changed, the red-veined cheeks were slacker over her bones, there was something old and stained about the skin around her eyes. Since he could remember, she had looked the same. She had come to Heype first when he was at the infant school, a boy who was soft in the head, five or six years old. One day she was not known, and the next she was there, push-ing the old pram for the first time along the beach. Old Beattie. Her cottage was half-way up the narrow lane leading to Church Steps, and they had all pelted past it, coming down from school, some of them slung tiny pebbles as they went by, hoping to hit her door or a window. Duncan had come afterwards, trailing behind them on his own. Beattie Thorpe had watched him.

'I know where she comes from,' his mother had said once, startling him. 'I remember her. You can't tell me about it. Don't you go talking to her.'

Occasionally, the two women had passed each other in the street and Duncan had waited, watching them both, aware of some recognition that flickered between them, though nothing was ever said. Old Beattie's eyes had narrowed. His mother had pulled him along.

'She was a funny one, then. She went her own way, went off, and that was that, we none of us saw her again. My mother knew Beattie Thorpe. Yes. But it's time enough ago. It's all past history.'

He could not discover more, and dared not ask, her words were like fragments of some other language.

When he was eleven or twelve, Old Beattie had saved his life. It was the beginning of December, early dark, with a thudding sky, the lights were on all the way down the town, as they came out of school. It was a Wednesday. He had to go and get the fish.

There were no men at all in the huts, the seas had

been too high, nobody had gone out that day. Duncan had walked, with anxiety mounting in him, from end to end of the row, time and again, going up to knock on the wooden doors, peering desperately into the small windows, expecting some miracle to occur, fish to be had from somewhere. The money for it was wrapped up inside greaseproof paper, and written on the paper was the note. It was the winter after his mother's accident.

The beach had darkened completely and the tide was high, crashing and foaming about the wooden stakes. He had almost cried, not knowing what she was going to say to him, or whether he should go to Todd's shop and buy the fish for supper there, or else to the grocer and ask them what he could take home, for the money she had given him But it was Wednesday, it was fish day, always, that was the way everything was planned and he was just learning about it, he dared not tamper now with the structure of their routine.

The wind had come roaring across the water, sending a sheet of spray slapping up into his face, blinding him.

When he opened his eyes again, they had been there. Four of them, and bigger than he was. He knew them all, knew their names and faces.

'Dafty! Dafty-Duncan!'

One of them had been Ted Flint.

The salt water was drying on his face in the wind, leaving the skin rough and sore, but his hair was still damp, hanging down coldly on his forehead. All of the huts were dark, there was nobody else at all on the beach. Duncan had stood, waiting for them. He was light enough, and did not resist. They tipped him over and caught him before he fell backwards on to the shingle, but they did not hurt him, as he expected, it was only their white faces that threatened him, their eyes glinting in the darkness. He remembered, now, how he had felt. It had been, simply nothing, complete blankness, he might have been dead, he was so afraid.

'Dafty-Duncan; Dafty-dafty-Duncan!' But they had sung in a chorus of whispers, their voices carried away to sea, no risk of being heard by anyone in the streets behind.

'Dafty-Duncan!'

They had spread out one of the mackerel nets and rolled him tightly in it, over and over, until he was a huge bundle. The nets smelled chokingly, of fish and oil and brine and tar, he could scarcely breathe. Then they had lifted him up and laid him in the bottom of one of the boats. After that, he heard their footsteps, running away over the stones and up on to the wall, thump-thump, thump-thump, and then gone. A single shout had come back to him through the darkness. After that, nothing. He was cramped with the cold, and the tightness of the hard, knotted net around him, and the bottom of the boat was wet, it came straight through his clothes.

After a moment he had opened his eyes. Humps of

cloud moving fast one close behind the other, in front of the moon. The waves crashed over, like cannons booming up the beach.

The water would not reach this far unless a storm got up, the boats were a always pulled high, close to the sea wall. But it had never occurred to him that he would do anything but die, he had lain rigid, arms pressing into his sides, the flesh of his hands bitten into by the mesh of the net, waiting. He had not cried out or spoken. The wind was howling.

Old Beattie had got him out. He never discovered how she had known where to find him, whether she had been somewhere down the beach and heard the noises. But, one moment there had been wind and sea and darkness, and then footsteps and the bump of the old pram, and her voice, shouting to him. He had not answered, only lay, she had come down all of the boats until she found him. Then she had climbed up and inside, he had watched the pale-pink rubber boots come over the edge. She had begun to unroll the nets. It took a long time. She looked into his face every so often, murmured something he could not catch, and when he was free of the net she had sat him up and chafed his hands between her own, and put them up to his raw face. She had taken him back to Tide Street, pushing him in the pram, among all the flotsam, the old newspapers. But when they got there, she would not wait, she was halfway back down the street by the time his mother had reached the door.

All over his body, the press of the nets had marked him in odd triangular patterns, so that he could not hide anything of what had happened from her, it had all come stammering out, scarcely coherent.

'Old Beattie,' he said, at the end, 'she came. Old Beattie.'

His mother had been strange towards him, at the same time angry and blaming and oddly tender. In the morning, she had waited for him to come into her bedroom to help her get up. Then she had said, 'You needn't start looking about for that old woman, that Beattie, and listening to any of her tales. You've cause to be grateful, and nothing more. She's funny, that one. She means nothing to you.'

But from time to time, ever since, he had disobeyed his mother, and walked some way along the beach with Beattie Thorpe, watching her eyes light upon something that glinted or obtruded from the pebbles, so that she stopped and darted down upon it like a jackdaw, and put it into the old pram. He had grown up and left school and gone to work at the Big House, and he still talked with her now and again. She had said to him, 'You know what's what, Duncan Pike, you're all right. You take no notice of what they say to you.' In the town, people had said that like called to like.

She never sought out his company, months went by without their meeting or stopping for one another, and he thought that was what she wanted, she was content to be on her own, trundling the old pram.

'I went away,' she said now. Her eyes were turquoise. 'They had me over at Ipswich, had me in the hospital. I've been away ill.'

He stared anxiously at her again, and he could see it, he was alarmed. She screwed her face up suddenly like a monkey, in an expression of self-derision.

'That's all done with,' she said, 'that's nothing. And what about Duncan Pike?'

'I'm all right.'

'You are?'

He waited. The water turned and turned.

'I could go away,' he said suddenly, and caught his breath, to hear the words spoken out loud.

Beattie Thorpe was still.

'To sea. Anywhere. I could.'

'And would you?'

He felt the words surging up inside him, and tried to choose the right ones, and not to stutter and stammer, because he needed to explain everything to her, about Cragg and the ships at Southampton and about the other thoughts he had had, way back, about how it had all begun. He wanted to bring Ted Flint into it, too, for he had always meant her to understand that the past made no difference, now, Ted Flint had been one of the boys who left him tied up in the boat, but that was done with, none of it mattered.

He could only say, 'I might do anything.'

'Well then. You make up your own mind, Duncan

Pike, you think about it and do as you choose. Are you listening?'

He shook his head slowly, the confusion was now so great.

'There's not many things you couldn't do, given you set yourself to it.'

But he was looking over her shoulder, back towards the lights of Heype, his face suddenly tight with worry. Beattie pulled up the collar of her old mac and shifted about inside the layer of newspapers, preparing to go.

'Yes,' she said, expressionlessly. 'There's all that.'

For she had seen how the boy's mother was with him. She knew Hilda Pike.

She let him, watched the careful way he walked ahead of her along the wall, pushing the old pram as he might push a child, or his mother in her wheelchair. He had very long, bony hands, he could do anything with them.

On the corner of Tide Street, she left him, trundling off with the raincoat flapping about her ankles. Duncan stood watching. Down one of the cuts between the tall houses, he heard the sea. I could go, he thought, I could go now, there are boats on the beach. I could take one. Frost glistened on the surface of the cobbles.

His mother would not speak to him. He asked her questions. 'Do you want your milk drink, yet? Have I to bank the fire? Is your bottle too hot?'

No reply. She scarcely looked at him. He felt weak with guilt and anxiety, he would have done anything at all to have her say something. It was vital to him to be back in her favour.

He went into the kitchen. It smelled of cold fat and frost on the stone floor, the damp wood of the draining board. He put the kettle on the black stove and waited for it to boil, he pulled back the rug and lifted her out of her chair and carried her upstairs, he laid her on the bed and helped her to undress, he drew the yellow curtains. Everything as usual, everything in the same order.

She was getting even thinner now, and her legs dangled uselessly like doll's legs, when he lifted her from the chair. She was very well, Doctor Nott said so, there was nothing whatsoever the matter with her, she ate well, and slept, though now it was with the help of tablets, she was strong, she might live for ever. It was only that she could not move her legs.

The pear log had gone out, one end almost burned away, charred and powdering, but the other end untouched, hard and green. Underneath, the fire was dead. It was very cold in the front room when he came in. She had not been able to lean down far enough to mend the fire, only to poke about in it with her stick.

'I went out,' he said, 'I only went out. I needed to walk, a bit. I do, don't I? You know. There's nothing wrong in it, I only went out.'

She sat motionless in the wheelchair.

'You wouldn't have liked to go. It's cold. It's freezing now, there's all ice in the puddles.'

The clock struck half-past ten. He had been gone a long time, then, much longer than he had meant. He had no sense of time, walking by the sea. 'There's that wall,' he went on, 'I heard you about the wall, I haven't forgotten, you needn't think. I could start it tomorrow. In the afternoon I could. I've to come home early, Cragg said. He wants me for Saturday, that's why. So tomorrow I'll do the wall, won't I?'

He talked to her that way, on and on, filled with dread by her silence, as he carried her up the stairs, got the things she needed, moved nervously about. When she was lying there, under the sheets and blankets, he stood for a moment, looking down. Her hair was thick and dry and flint-grey, scraped back tightly from her forehead in the daytime, and held with a metal comb. Now, she had loosened it and it waved slightly about her face, softening the line of bone and making her look younger. But she was not young, he thought that she could never have been young. He knew nothing about her.

As a child, he had always told her everything, had needed to make endless confessions. The urge to do so welled up in him now, he wanted to go and kneel down beside her bed, and say, I thought I could go away, I wanted to go away and I went out to the tower, I talked to Old Beattie, I wish I were like Ted Flint, *he* went away, and he came back. *Why?* I could go away.

He said nothing. She turned her face away from him, on the pillow

'That's everything,' Duncan said. 'You've all you want now, haven't you?'

He waited for a second, and then walked out of the room. He knew that she had moved her head again, to watch him, and he felt pride, because he had not told her. He had kept something back, and now, he would go on doing it. Everything was changing. There's not many things you couldn't do,' Beattie had said.

Downstairs, he went into the kitchen and brewed himself tea, and then sat in front of the dead fire, holding the china mug between his hands tightly, wide awake with excitement.

Though, in the morning, he could not remember it, and his mother still did not speak to him.

By twelve o'clock, he had finished digging over the old flower-bed and raking the soil finely, it was ready for planting. Cragg came down and looked it over, but he only nodded, surly, the talk about Southampton forgotten. A wind was getting up again, after the previous night's calm, a sharp wind, coming in quick gusts and making the sea choppy and flecked with white, running fast.

Duncan left the Big House and went down to Whick's, Builders, to buy cement and sand and whitewash for the wall.

His mother had sat and eaten her breakfast and

then written the note, handing it over to him without a word and watching until he had put it away in his pocket. He had taken it up to the Big House, and burned it in Cragg's bonfire, behind the compost, stirring the ashes over with his foot to make them disintegrate.

'That's heavy flow, young Duncan Pike, that weighs half a ton, cement, you'll not carry it.'

But he had forced himself to lift and settle it on his back, though he was bent almost double, going out of the builder's yard, the bones of his neck and spine were aching and burning. He could not see or hear the men behind him, only guess at what they said. It was important to do as they did, to manage an impossibly heavy load, without difficulty.

'That'll drop off.'

'He's not so daft, that one,' Whick said, 'he'll do.'

'What?' John Dent shook his head and went back to loading grey roof slates on to the truck, his eyes wide with disbelief. Dafty-Duncan! Since he was a boy, he had heard his mother and his aunt talking to him very loudly, when he came into the shop, putting the loaf of bread under his arm and guiding him like a blind person, out of the door.

'Carry it carefully, hold it tight, Duncan. Go straight home, now.'

'What do you shout at him for? He's not deaf.'

His mother had shrugged, unloading a fresh tray of bread. 'He's not the same as you, you've got to make allowances. You have to be sure he understands you, that's all.'

And now, today, he had come stammering into the yard and stood about, his hands and arms never still, eyes huge in the pale, bony face, buying sand and cement and stubbornly heaving it home.

John Dent grinned, piling up the slates, remembering how they had been as kids, the things they had said and done to Dafty-Duncan.

When he reached the cottage and dropped the sack on to the garden, he could scarcely stand upright again, his muscles were like pulled ropes. He did not go inside. She was in the front room, waiting, he could see the shape of her through the net curtains. He turned and walked deliberately away along Tide Street and down one of the alleys.

As he passed by the side of the Ship, the door swung open and shut behind Ted Flint.

Duncan stopped dead. Ted Flint came easily towards him, head cocked back, ears very red, just below the rim of his woollen hat. Bits of blond hair fronded out and over the collar of his jersey. Ted Flint. Duncan could see the tattoos, a rose, an anchor, a bird, a linked pair of hearts, up his thick forearms. He began to move away, towards the lifeboat.

'Well then?' Ted Flint said. Duncan could feel him coming up behind him, head and shoulders taller.

'All right are you, Duncan Pike?'

Duncan stiffened

'Hey?'

'Yes,' he said quickly. 'Yes. All right.'

For some reason, Ted Flint laughed. He was look-ing at Duncan. But it was not a vicious laugh, there was nothing behind it. Duncan thought, I could be like him, that's how I ought to be. Ted Flint was every-thing. Sometimes he spoke, sometimes half-nodded. Often, nothing. But today, he kept pace with Duncan, going across the shingle towards his boat. Sky and sea and beach were all the same colour, merging together and oddly pearled. The breeze had freshened, raising a swell.

They reached the blue and white boat. Duncan thought, this is all I want, I want to stay here. The rest of the men were still at their dinners, or else further off, in the last of the huts.

Ted Flint walked off to the water's edge and stood, gazing down, then lifted his head to measure the waves, tracing them back. The wind was south-east, rolling the sea slant-ways on to the beach.

Duncan thought of nothing, not his aching back or his mother waiting for him to go home and start on the broken wall, nothing. He would stay here for as long as Ted Flint would let him, content with any-thing. It was a long time, now, since he had so much as spoken.

Ted Flint wandered back up to the boat, hands in his pockets. He looked like all the others, now, Duncan saw, younger, but old, too, broad and slow and careful, easygoing or evil-tempered whichever he chose. He looked at Duncan, and his blunt features were luminous with some secret amusement.

'Want to come out in the boat then, Duncan Pike?'

Out. Out in the boat. He was taking the boat out, he would let him come. Duncan could not begin to speak or to think clearly, it was scarcely believable, what Ted Flint had said. 'Want to come out?' Out. In the boat. He would climb in and sit there and they would go, take the nets four or five miles, and then fish along the sandbank, they would disappear on to the sea. He had never been.

Ted Flint paused for a second and then turned and began to get ready, hailing to one of the other men to help him, taking the rust-stained fishing hooks up from where they lay on the beach, and the lines, and luminous orange floats, loosening the cable. Without warning, he began to give Duncan orders, as Cragg did: do this, move that, lift it, let it go, hold it, and Duncan obeyed, transfixed, desperate to please. The other man left them, to walk slowly beside the waterline, smoking his pipe.

The boat was down and ready, the motor running. Ted Flint was standing up in it, towering above Duncan, tall as a king.

'Get in then, if you're coming.'

Why should he take me out there, Duncan thought. *Why?* I've never been, I don't know anything, he doesn't speak to me, why should he ask me to go? Though he could sense no animosity in Ted Flint, no threat of danger. He was entirely puzzled.

A wave gathered, battleship-grey and seething along its crest, and then crashed over. The boat lifted and rocked.

'Hey?'

There was a moment when Duncan was ready to spring forwards and up, when he could already feel himself going out to sea, imagine the movement of it beneath him, they were pushing ahead. 'Want to come out in the boat then?' With Ted Flint. *I could go.*

And then another wave began to gather, and suddenly, he saw them coming at him, one after the next, rising up higher and higher, ready to break about his head and drag him down into them, and he knew that once they had pushed the boat out, then there would be no escape for him, he would be alone with Ted Flint, towering above him, in the middle of the endless sky and heaving sea, and he was seized with choking panic, he turned and began to run, pounding off down the beach to get away from the menace of the waves and wind, and the chugging of the boat, out of the reach of Ted Flint, he would have done anything rather than go on that sea.

'That's not safe, you'd never manage, you'd not know what to do. You leave going in boats alone.'

He reached the steps and scrambled up and raced over the square, making for the dark, close safety of

Wash Alley. Later, he would think of the folly of it, and want to claw at himself in helpless anger, later, he would ask again and again what Ted Flint had thought and said, know that there would never in his life be a second chance. He had not dared to go out in a boat, he had been overcome with terror at the sight of the sea, he had run away. So what they said about him was true.

Now, he only wanted to be home, he threw himself in through the door of the cottage and stood in the front room, beside the high oak dresser, panting and shaking, his breath and blood pushing like waves against the thin walls of his chest.

His mother still sat, in the wheelchair, close beside the window, looking out. After a moment she said, 'Now what have they been doing to you? Now what?'

Duncan leaned his arms upon the dresser and wept, because he had escaped from the sea, and was sick with shame at himself, and because his mother had spoken to him.

All afternoon, he rebuilt the wall. The old mortar crumbled away in his hands, and when he knocked it off the individual bricks, it blew up into his face with the powder of the whitewash, making his eyes smart. He worked very slowly. Cragg had taught him how to do a job. The whole wall had to be pulled down, to the bottom layer of brick, it would take far longer than this one afternoon, perhaps even longer than the weekend.

When he bent his back, the muscles hurt between his shoulders. From the window, behind the net curtains, his mother watched him.

After his fit of crying had stopped, he had not answered her question, he had said nothing at all about what had happened. It had become, within a few days, the most important thing with him, not to do so, never to tell her anything again.

She had followed him into the back kitchen.

'What have they done to you? Who was it? What have they said?'

He began to take eggs out of the wicker basket on the table but she had driven the chair hard across the kitchen towards him, slapping down his hands. 'You leave that to me, I'll do that. You're not in any state, not for anything, look at you.'

Duncan pushed his hands deep inside his pockets to stop the trembling. His mother set the bowl on her lap and broke the eggs into it and began to beat them.

'I don't know what's happened to you, Duncan Pike, I don't. Something's happening. You mind what you're about, these days. You're not a baby now, are you? You'll go the way they all said you'd go, you'll just play into their hands, won't you? Losing your temper, crashing out of the house, crashing in again, fits and tantrums. You try and keep a hold on yourself. You're not a baby, you've to learn things. You mind what you're about.'

He wanted to ask her what she expected of him, for

in the past it had always seemed to be so little, she had told him over and over again the things he could not, would never be able, to do, had told him that he could not expect life to treat him as it treated others. Expect nothing from yourself.

Now, he was groping towards all the new possibilities, they shimmered just ahead, he could see them, and hear them inside his own head, he wanted everything. But she told him to mind himself, to be careful, told him he would not manage, and at the same time, that it was the other people, they were the ones who shook their heads and expected nothing of him. He was behaving now, as they had all waited for him to behave.

But it's you, Duncan said, it is you, it is you, you, and struck the trowel hard down the edge of a brick, so that it went on, into his hand. The knuckles, already sore and stiff with cold, spouted little beads of blood in a long line. He scarcely hesitated and did not look up, for she must not see what had happened, he would not do anything about it. It was his own fault.

When he was almost five, she had taken him, once only, and for some unspoken reason of her own, up to the swings in the small children's playground, at the top of the town. Nobody else had been there.

'Push,' she had told him. 'Push with your legs. You don't need me to do everything for you, there's something you can do for yourself. *Push.*'

Very awkwardly, he had learned how to bend his

knees back and then forwards again, to the rhythm of the swing, until he began to go higher, without meaning it, too high, the sky had lurched about and he had been filled with dread.

'Get off now,' he said, and the swing had rocked a little, he was sitting at an angle on the wooden plank, unbalancing it. 'Off now, off.' He was still unable to talk clearly, only she could understand him. 'Off, now.'

She had done nothing, only stood, as though wanting him to fall, or as though she might be unaware of him, were thinking of something else, in some other place. She was wearing the bottle-green coat with the beige fur collar, the same coat she had always worn.

He had screamed, to try and bring her back to 'Off now, get off, get off, *get off....*'

In his agitation he had fallen, not far or badly, only the palms of his hands were grazed, but he had seen the black ground coming up to meet him, had felt the bump and the jarring and expected all the bones to come pushing out in every direction, through his own flesh, he had screamed with the shock of it.

She had waited, had not picked him up or spoken to him, only stood, staring blankly ahead of her and kneading her fingers inside her coat pockets, until he got himself up.

'All that screaming!' she said at last, pulling him away by the hand. 'All that. You're not hurt, that was nothing. They don't want that when they have you at the school, I'll tell you. That screaming. No. We won't come here again, will we?'

And they had not, to Duncan's relief, swinging had been one more thing that he could not do. It seemed to him that she had one of her lists hidden somewhere about her, to which she added, each day, his new failures. There were trials set for him and he did not pass. When he hurt himself, she was cold towards him, sometimes getting plaster or ointment or disinfectant out, but angrily, as though he were to blame. Yet he remembered a fever, once, when he had lain in bed with terrible nightmares, clinging like bats to the inside walls of his head, and then he had woken to find her sitting on the painted wooden chair, close up to his pillow, her face full of anxiety, holding his hand. He had been more than ever bewildered, wondering why he should suddenly merit her kindness. Later, he had thought about it carefully, and seen that he was to blame only for accidents, for the cuts and bruises that came with bumps or falls.

After that, he went in trepidation about the world, holding himself in, avoiding every conceivable object of danger. He watched the others riding bicycles in Market Street and swarming up the martello tower, and wading out into the middle of one of the streams, looking for fish, and he caught his breath for them, terrified by their physical ease and struck dumb by the pressure of his need to warn them, warn them. Your own fault, he would have said, listen, listen, it will be your own fault, you will be to blame, nobody will help you.

Then, a boy had fallen from some railings in the school yard, upside down on to his head, and that had been his own fault, that was an accident, the ambulance had come and taken him to hospital and he had been there for three weeks. But they had all been told to write the boy letters, they had brought gifts for him and made up a class story, and Duncan must do drawings, because he could not write. Once again, he was thrown into confusion. A boy had fallen, he had been to blame, and yet the teacher, Miss Napp, said, 'Everyone must think of something specially nice for Malcolm, poor Malcolm, everyone must be kind to him.'

In silence, Duncan had drawn his drawing and shut his mind off from the impossible questions, his pencil moving round and round and round.

So that, when he cut the blade of the trowel across his cold knuckles, he shook the blood off and then pressed his hand briefly against his coat. That was all, for he was to blame, he would say nothing.

All afternoon, he thought of Ted Flint, out fishing in the blue and white boat. He could hear the sea tossing about, at the end of Wash Alley. His own fear of it had been a shock to him, for he had never seen the waves in such a light before, he had liked them, walked by them, he had wanted the sea to take him away. He could swim, it was not that, for they had all gone to the small pool up by the tennis courts, when he was in Class V, and he had not found it difficult, after a while, to push his limbs out across the water, he had never thought to be frightened.

'You listen, Duncan Pike. You don't go swimming in that river, and you don't go in the sea. Never mind the others, they're different, they've nothing to do with you. It's not safe, you wouldn't manage. You go in the water at the pool when they take you, and that's all.'

But he had never thought of disobeying her, for the others went down to swim in the river all together and they did not offer to take Duncan.

He stirred the cement about and then ladled it thickly on to the flat brick. Ted Flint, he thought, Ted Flint. I could have gone.

When he could bear it no longer, he put the trowel down on the wall and went, he had to see whether the boat was back.

At first, there was nothing, as far as he could see on the heaving, steely water. A fine rain had started, blowing into his face from off the sea. He stood by one of the stakes, screwing his eyes up to look ahead. Then, out of nowhere, the boat appeared, coming in fast towards the shore and pitching, like a train on a switchback. Ted Flint was standing up, his bright yellow oilskin like a beacon against the sky.

Down at the water's edge, Davey Ward stood, waving his arms up and down to guide the boat in. It would have been all right, Duncan thought, he's here, he has come back. It would. I could have gone. He wanted to cry, and he wanted to go and hide in the alleys, out of sight of Ted Flint's eyes, the jeers of the other men. But he did not move, he stayed, looking on, needing to be by the sea.

The boat came in on the swell of a wave, and there was the scrape of the wood grazing to a halt on sand and shingle. Duncan saw the water streaming down off Ted Flint's oilskins. His bare hands were purple as plums, laying down the planks to guide the boat up. Someone shouted from the huts and he shouted back, but the words were lost on the wind. Duncan thought, they are friends, they help him, men shouting like that to one another, asking questions and answering, knowing the right things to say. I could have gone, they would have been shouting down to me.

He pictured the inside of the huts, and himself, standing there, and drinking tea and rum, his own red hands around the steaming mug, being one of the others. There was nothing else he wanted.

The cut from the trowel throbbed across his bare knuckles. It was raining harder, his mother would be wanting tea. He thought suddenly of how much he left her alone. But he would have changed that, some way, if he could, and she had never let him. 'Mrs Ward might come,' he had told her, in the weeks after her accident, 'Mrs Napp sent this ... Mrs Carr asked ... Old Beattie would push you out ... Mrs Ward might come ....'

But she would have none of them. Send them away, don't answer the door, don't take it, no, no, we don't need them, we can manage. And she had taught him to manage, the house and caring for her, and then his job at the Big House, after he left school.

'Blood's thicker than water . .. . We keep ourselves to ourselves in this town.... You're not my son for nothing, Duncan Pike.'

Besides, he was too young, and simple, she said, if anyone came and sat with her in his place, what good would that do, where would he go? 'I bore you, I bred you, you'd not have managed anything, without me.'

So he should go back to her now. He wondered what things went on inside his mother's head, as she sat all day in her wheelchair, doing the white crochet. He did not know what comparison there might be with others, or with himself, and his own muddled thoughts and feelings, she mended a hammock or dug over the Big House garden, he did not know anything about any other people.

He should go back now. There was a fine cobweb of raindrops over his jersey, clinging to the hairs on the surface of the wool.

'You're a case, Duncan Pike! Daft beggar!'

Ted Flint had come out of the hut again, and down the beach towards him.

'You!'

But he spoke mildly enough. 'That's only a bit

choppy,' he said now, looking at the sea. 'Nothing to hurt you.'

Duncan looked up, rubbing his fingers anxiously about on the wooden stake. Ted Flint's expression was strange to him, sharp and mocking, but at the same time friendly, genial, as though none of it mattered.

'You'd be all right on the boat, you'd do, give yourself half a chance. I'd shape you.'

He said nothing.

'That's getting up now, though.' The sky was darkening.

'Want a fish for your tea then, our Duncan?'

His eyes were wide open, glinting with amusement. Duncan felt wary, remembering. But it was Ted Flint.

'It's not .... I can't. No. Wednesday's fish day, we buy our fish on Wednesdays.'

'Not *buy*. I asked you if you wanted a fish, not buy it. I'm giving you one, aren't I?'

He walked off, back into the hut, and came out again a moment later, standing on the step and holding out a package. 'Hey up, then!' Duncan hesitated, then made his way very slowly across the shingle. In two of the other huts, he could see lights on, the shadows of the men, knew that they watched him.

'Herring that is, make you grow up a big lad.'

After a moment, Duncan took the parcel. The paper was wet already from the fish inside.

'Come out and catch it yourself,' Ted Flint said, 'next time.'

Duncan turned. His limbs felt queerly heavy, and his head light, his ears singing. He had to make an effort to lift his feet up and put them down again, to get himself over the shingle. He carried the newspaper parcel just as Ted Flint had given it to him, flat across his outstretched hands. Next time, he had said, come and catch it for yourself next time. Next time, next time, next time....

When he reached the cottage and stood beside the unfinished wall in the drizzle, he remembered that he had not thanked Ted Flint for the fish.

In the hut, Davey Ward said, 'You want looking at,' drinking his tea, 'you and all. You'll do no good there, I can tell you.'

Ted Flint shrugged, grinning. 'I'm not bothered.'

'He's a case, that's what. Him and his mother. You're wasting your time.'

Ted Flint kicked his boot against the bench. 'Yes,' he said. 'That mother. Bloody old witch.'

'What's it to you, then?'

'Nothing. No.'

'Get him in your boat, he'd be lost, he'd be like an animal, you'd lose him over the side, that's what. He's not fit.'

'He's all right.'

'Never.'

'He's *all right*, I said. There's no harm in him.'

'No harm, no. I never said so, did I? Harm. But he's

like a baby, he's frightened of his own shadow, you see that. There's nothing up here, nothing inside. He'd never manage.'

'He manages.'

'Does what Hilda Pike tells him.'

'Yes.'

'Well, and without her, then? Nothing. He'd do *nothing*, he'd be finished, they'd have to send him away, they'd put him in a home.'

'No.'

'They would.'

'He'd do.' Ted Flint stepped to the door and slung out the dregs of his tea mug, looked at the sky. 'Getting up a bit now.'

'I don't know what you bother for.' Davey Ward stood up. 'All of a sudden.'

'It does no harm.'

'You leave well alone, take my advice. You'll only make trouble. She wants nothing and nobody, that woman.'

'Her! It's not her, is it?'

'We tried. All of us. We tried years ago. You wouldn't remember.'

'I do.'

'Leave well alone. You take him on, there'll be trouble.' Davey Ward walked out of the hut. 'Ask your own mother.'

'It's nothing.' Ted Flint turned away. 'I'm not that bothered, you needn't take on.'

Though he thought of the peaky, child's face of Duncan Pike, and felt sorry enough for him, would have done something. It didn't matter. He locked the door of the hut and picking up his bicycle swung a leg over. It was still raining.

*

In the cottage on Tide Street, Hilda Pike made him drop the fish, still wrapped up, into the dustbin.

'We eat our fish Wednesday,' she said. 'We buy what we want and we take nothing, not from anyone. You know.'

He had smelled the beginning of the storm the previous day, as the others had. The wind had been driving blizzards inland, down the county, to the west. Now, that morning, turning to look back at the top of Church Hill, Duncan saw the sky. Over the sea, there was still a wash of light blue, the horizon glinted. But the sun had risen out of a red sky, and above the river, the clouds were massing together, liver-coloured, the marshes were dark as iron. Duncan felt uneasy. But the wind was still only roughening the surface of the sea.

By lunchtime it had veered round abruptly and begun to blow a gale. Duncan could barely stand against it, he moved in closer to the shed. Cragg had set him on to sawing wood. Snow came in flurries for five or ten minutes at a time, hard and stinging against his face, and then was carried off again on the wind.

Cragg ate through his sandwiches and drank his tea, said nothing at all. They had tied the door to, with a piece of string. The Big House was empty, Mrs Reddingham-Lee had gone away.

Down the slopes, in the houses of Heype, window-sashes began to loosen, the panes bumping softly, front gates rammed hard shut. Duncan went back to his logs. Half an hour later, the sky was dense as stone, and the red roof of the Big House was thick with gulls, making inland from the sea. At four, the town was almost dark. The sea was racing in fast, the waves coming down harder and harder on to the beach. The huts were almost empty. Nobody had been out all day. Davey Ward fiddled with a sprat net and hovered in his hut doorway, looking at the sky.

Coming into the shed where Duncan was putting the saw away, ready for home, Cragg said, 'Be rough tonight.'

Duncan was suddenly afraid. Every winter he dreaded the storms, because of the noise they made, the tearing and crashing, but most of all he was afraid simply of his own fear, at what they might do. He had watched the animals, seen cats flatten back their ears and slink away close to the walls, and the dogs lifting up their heads without warning, to howl. All over the marshes now, seabirds were coming in, they huddled together in the lee of old rowing-boats, and among the clumps of reed, and inland, wild hares raced for shelter among the gorse, fur flying.

He had always waited for their cottage to be washed away, he had imagined the great waves thundering down and tearing the bricks up like roots of a tooth, sucking the whole street up inside itself. For it had happened, people talked about it. Once, Tide Street had been quite far back, almost in the centre of the town, and through various terrible winters, and spring tides, the land had crumbled away, whole streets had dissolved like paper and the sea had sluiced over and flooded the river and the marshes for miles, inland. In summer, he walked along the defence wall on clear, still nights, and thought of it, of the houses lying at the bottom of the sea, of chairs and tables and beds and ornaments which had been valuable to people, and of the cold steeples of churches. Though it was hard to remember what the storms were like then, when the air was warm under the risen moon.

Turning out of Market Street, he was almost lifted up and sent spinning, by the gale. The awning over Lunt's pie shop rattled, loose from one of its chains.

He dared not go and look at the sea, he could hear it booming on the shingle, the spray was blowing down Wash Alley into his face. His legs went weak suddenly, as he thought of the great press of waves beating up towards the house, and of how fragile everything was, rock and brick and the bones of people, fine as splinters against the force of it. He thought of the whole of England, as he had seen it on maps, spilled completely over by the sea, the edges eaten away like a biscuit, smaller and smaller and then swallowed, there would be no trace left. His mind sheered away from it, and he opened the door and was pushed hard by the wind behind him, into the front room.

On the beach, Davey Ward stood beside the lifeboat for a moment, lifted his hand up to touch the polished wood. Already the waves were high up beyond the stakes, roaring over the last shelf of pebbles, and the tide had two hours to go.

In the coastguard station, Joss Flack made a circle on a chart, looked at the direction of the arrows, and then out to sea again, rubbed his thumbs about over the pads of his fingers, waited. All afternoon, the trawlers had been moving fast along the horizon, making for port.

A wave lifted and toppled, and the foam seethed about the breakwater, the windows of the lookout were mizzled with spray.

In the cottage at the top of King Lane, Ted Flint stirred, straightening and recrossing his legs, listening to the gale, over the sound of music on the television. Just before eight, he went out.

Black and White minstrels strutted and danced, and Alice Flint went on watching them and knitting, blank-eyed, thinking of nothing.

Inland, power cables came down, the lights went out in farmhouses and cottages out beyond Heype. As

Ted Flint walked down the hill towards the Ship Inn, it began to sleet.

'You're to cut your toe-nails tonight,' Hilda Pike said, 'after you've had a bath.'

Duncan's hand was still for a second, holding the reel of thin cotton he used to make the rigging. The radio played Viennese Waltzes from the Palm Court. She would not have a television set inside the cottage.

The ship was five and a half inches high and almost finished. It weighed nothing, balanced on his hand. He soaked the labels off matchboxes, saved for him by Cragg and Old Beattie and Mrs Reddingham-Lee, and then razored the wood finely, and used spent matches themselves, too, varnished and painted. The sails worked by a system of thread pulleys, each one could be individually raised and lowered. He was working from a picture of the *Victory*, torn from a magazine he had found beside the dustbins at the Big House.

'Did you hear?'

'Wine, Woman and Song' came waltzing out of the radio ballroom.

'It's time,' she said, 'it's past nine o'clock. You get the water boiling, leave that thing alone, now, I'm not having you slovenly in your habits. And you can do your hair, at the same time.'

There was a rushing noise inside his head, it came up fast to the surface and boiled over, and he smashed his fist down like a chopper, crushing the tiny wood and cotton model, like a thin-winged fly, between itself and the table. Everything in the room shook slightly, and then resettled. Beyond the window, in Tide Street, the roar of the gale and the sea.

Hilda Pike did not speak.

Eventually, he lifted his hand up very gently and began to detach the broken pieces from where they had stuck to his palm. The edge of a splinter had sunk into the pulpy flesh at the base of his thumb. He took no notice of it. When he had gathered everything up together, he cupped his hand to the edge of the table and swept the bits and threads into it, and then walked two steps across the room, to drop them into the blazing centre of the fire. They vanished in a single lick of flame. Then the log burned on.

Hilda Pike's fingers flick-flick-flicked ceaselessly in and out of the crochet.

'You think I've forgotten.' She did not look up at him. 'Or else you've forgotten. But I haven't. I don't forget. You think I don't know, but I knew how it would be from way back. I knew. I'd only to look at your face.'

He had not moved, he was still looking down into the fire. 'They sent you home from school. They put a note in your pocket and they sent you home with it. Weren't going to have that, were they? And can you blame them? And I had to go up there and talk them round, into taking you back. Yes, you may have forgotten, but I never shall. I knew. You can't change, you'll never change, not inside yourself. You don't try, Duncan Pike.'

His head was clear, as though it had been rinsed through with ice-cold water, everything was sharper and brighter, her voice echoed like thin, high shouts, through a cave.

He had not forgotten.

There had been big glass jars of paint, and he was allowed to spoon some of it and set it around the edges of the old plate, one thick blob at a time, he might have any colours he liked, but no more than three. They painted, once a fortnight only, everything else was cleared off the low tables, and over their own clothes they wore special old shirts, made for the school by the mother of Miss Napp.

He could draw all day, filling page after page, using pencil after pencil, he would go on, never lifting his eyes up, not hearing if they told him to stop. But the paint alarmed him, it was something entirely different, looser and more slippery, something he could never quite control. He always bent down very close to the paper, and used the end of the brush, finely pointed like a pencil, to make little, elaborate marks, working in a single small corner. The others gouged out violent colours and spread them on like jam, bending the bristles of their paint-brushes and rubbing it all about.

But only three colours at a time. He had stood in silence, knowing what he wanted and overcome by the largeness of the glass pots and the bright white and blue, the emerald and nasturtium and scarlet, so that in the end Miss Napp had lost patience and told him which to choose, and helped him to them, blob, blob, blob, on the china plate, like runny ice-cream.

He had wanted to paint a haystack. Last week, they had all gone by bus out to a farm near Bloxhall, and he had seen one, it was the only thing he could, for certain, remember the shape of. He wanted to make a haystack, square and yellow and huge as a house, over all the sheet of paper, a haystack on green grass under a sky-blue sky.

He stared down at the china plate. Miss Napp had given him white and black and purple.

For a long time he stared, and did not know what he might do, he was entirely bewildered, unable to make new plans on the ruins of the old ones. And then he had lifted the plate and brought it down upon the table, smash, smash, smash, and knocked the pieces off, ground his feet again and again into them, so that the white and black and purple slurred together and came off on the crepey soles of his sandals in a dark mess, mixed up with chips of the china. They had sent him home, with a note in his pocket, and he had never done anything like it again, never behaved violently except in secret, beating the rushes down or grinding two pebbles viciously together, somewhere by himself.

Now, the ship model was broken and burned.

'I don't know what's happening, Duncan Pike. Something's happening. I watch you. I know your face.'

He bent down and took up another pear log and laid it carefully, at an angle, across the fire. The draught raced over the room from under the front door, sending the flames up at once, to cradle round it, catching the bark alight.

He said, 'I'd best put the kettle on, then.'

Hilda Pike did not reply. Then, there were the footsteps, and a rapping upon the door.

Ted Flint was like a giant in the front room, Duncan saw him beside the oak dresser and it seemed to him that he would be able to lift his hand and bring it down and crush them entirely, as he himself had just crushed the ship model.

His mother had gone still, the crochet resting on her lap, her eyes hard and bright as beads.

Ted Flint laughed. 'I thought, why not take Duncan? Get the lad out for an hour.' He looked across the room. 'Are you coming then? I'll buy you a jar, our Duncan, down at the Ship.'

Duncan's eyes widened. He did not move. Someone might have struck him a blow on the side of the head. Ted Flint's voice came and went like the sea, faded very far away. But his first instinct was to be afraid, to try and discover a reason. What had happened, all of a sudden? Come out in the boat. Come down to the

Ship. Why? He was not to blame, yet it all seemed to have begun inside himself. Why? Though the rest of him would have done anything, gone anywhere, would trust Ted Flint entirely.

'Have an hour off,' he said. 'Why not? It's a rough night.'

Music still came from the radio, a man's voice singing about a Merry Donkey.

'Come on, get your coat on, Duncan, why don't you?'

There was the same air of amusement about him, the same look, smoothed over his face like butter. Duncan thought, he doesn't care, he's not afraid of her, he can stand there and look down at her and she is nothing. And it seemed to him more than ever bewildering, that Ted Flint was as he was and had been away but come back, and now he stayed here in Heype, free as a bird.

'Hey?'

For a second, there was nothing, there was silence, even from the beating of the gale. Then, Hilda Pike had launched herself forward, the wheelchair was spinning across the room towards Ted Flint, and she had her stick up, waving it at him, beating it in the air, so that Duncan thought she would have rammed it into his face. Her voice was rising higher and higher as she spoke, raucous as a bird. Duncan shrank back against the wall in shame and terror. 'You get away from here, Ted Flint, you get out, don't you bring yourself into this house again. Leave us alone, you leave us alone. Get out!'

Ted Flint stood his ground, though Duncan could see his body tensed under the oilskins, wondered what he might do.

'He doesn't go drinking, he doesn't go anywhere, does he? Who do you think you're asking, Ted Flint? You know about him. He's nothing to do with any of you.'

She was pressed up against him in her chair, and now she jabbed the stick forwards, it would have gone into his thighs. 'You get out, don't you come banging on this door again, making trouble. You leave him be.'

Ted Flint lifted a hand, took hold of the stick and twisted it lightly out of her grasp, then threw it, at floor level, across the room. It skidded to rest underneath the window.

'It's what you need, boy,' he said quietly, 'I tell you. Get your coat on, I'll buy you a jar.'

He spoke in the same, slow, laughing voice. He did not care, Hilda Pike might not have been there, he thought nothing of her. She turned the wheelchair round in a half-circle, to face Duncan. The bass voice sang out roundly from the wireless.

'You go out of here with him, Duncan Pike, and you don't come back.' He knew that she meant it. None of them spoke again.

When Ted Flint opened the door, Duncan thought the sea had come up into the garden, everything was roaring. He shrank away, back towards the kitchen door.

After a long time, he looked up at her. She had not moved in the chair. Now she reached out a hand and pointed to where her stick lay under the window on the floor. Her face was grey-white, her eyes oddly distended, and as though they had sunk further back in her head. Duncan went across the room slowly, and got the stick.

'You can take me to bed, now. You can do it before your bath. I'm ready to go to bed. My back hurts.'

He handed the stick to her and took the rug off her knees, and folded it, and then lifted his mother very gently, carried her upstairs.

'You're mad!'

'You can tell him.' Davey Ward tapped the stem of his pipe against his front teeth. 'I have, I've told him, over and again. He's wasting his time and he'll lay up trouble. Why bother? What's it all in aid of, I want to know? All of a sudden. *I've* told him. You may as well save your breath.'

Ted Flint raised the mug of beer and drank from it easily.

'What's it all about?'

'Nothing,' he said. 'Nothing special.'

'You ask Old Beattie Thorpe. She knows, she'll tell you. Knew her as a girl, knew the family. She'd tell you.'

'No.'

'No – well, mind yourself, then.'

Ted shook his head, still laughing. The bar was full of men now, the air thick with pipe smoke.

'You'd lose him in here, that young Duncan, he'd slip down a crack in the table, like half of him slipped down his mother's leg, day he was born. He'd not know what to do with himself.'

'He'd learn.'

Davey Ward hissed. Beyond the windows, across the square. the sea.

'A foreigner, he was,' Bert Malt said.

'What?'

'That Duncan Pike's father.'

'So they say.' Ted Flint had never believed it.

'Oh yes. Came off one of the trawlers at Lowestoft. Ask Old Beattie,'

'With Hilda Pike? Never!'

'She'd legs to use in those days, hadn't she?'

'Get on.'

'There's plenty up there that knew her. He's only your age, Ted Flint, it's not so long ago.'

'Long enough.'

'Well, he was a foreigner, They're not fussy.'

'He'd not need to be.'

Ted Flint lifted a fresh glass of beer. 'She is,' he said. 'She'd be fussy.'

Davey Ward stood up. The others waited. 'I'll go out and take a look at it.'

They parted for him, standing back from the draught as the door opened.

Ted Flint went over to the darts board, forgetting about Duncan Pike, waiting, like the rest, for high water, for what the storm might do. But, coming here, along Tide Street, he had remembered her face as she came at him across the tiny room. He thought, she'd kill you. Or him. She'd take that stick to anyone. She would.

Davey Ward came back inside, hair and face streaming with water. He took the pipe, still lighted, out of his pocket again, said nothing. Ted Flint sent the dart off and into the board, for a double.

He waited until she had gone to sleep. But she was tired, she had slipped down between the heavy blankets like some frail insect, it was hardly any time.

As he pulled on the raincoat and boots and woollen gloves, he was trembling, his heart thudded when he bent down. He wore nothing on his head, and when he got outside he hunched himself up, leaning forwards into the gale. All the way there, he stayed close to the wall.

The Ship stood back from the square, behind the lifeboat memorial, open to the sea. It was crashing up high over the defence wall, now, the noise was like thunder, the air heavy with sleet and blown spume.

He skirted round the back of the pub, his rubber

boots silent and slippery on the cobbles, and then on the belt of muddy grass. When he came up to the bar window, he pressed himself as hard as he could against the wall, edging up step by small step, nearer to the light.

At first, he could see nothing for the flying mist in the air, and hear nothing above the gale. He waited, shivering. He thought, I could have gone with him, he asked me, he came for me, I could have gone. Though he scarcely believed it.

Then the sounds began to detach themselves, a wave of laughter and a single voice calling across the bar, somebody banging. The low room was brown-yellow, and all the men were blue, their shadows falling darkly together across tables and walls and floor. He saw Ted Flint's back, the fair hair curling low over his collar.

He could not have gone in, not even in Ted Flint's company, the sight of all the men there together terrified him, he smelled the strange smell of the place even from the outside, like an animal scenting danger. He would not have been able to stand there or speak or move. But he had had the chance.

He took his hand out of his pocket and held it against the brick, pressing it, trying to feel the warmth from within. He thought, I could do anything.

In the cottage on Tide Street, Hilda Pike slept.

Later, when he did come home, cold and stiff from holding his body so hard to the wall, he boiled the kettles and bathed himself in the tin bath, as she had told him.

They had been expecting it, all of them. Davey Ward had gone uneasily to sleep, downstairs on the sofa, keeping his clothes on, and there were others, too, all about the town. In the coastguard station, Joss Flack moved his hand every so often, towards the telephone, silent in its black cradle, heard bells that did not ring, and saw imaginary flames hurtle up into the tossing sky.

The tide lashed up and over the defence wall, spilling across the street and slavering like tongues down between the alleys, and then it turned back, furiously into itself. It began to snow, the flakes caught up and whirled about crazily by the gale.

Duncan woke seconds before he heard the boom of the first, and then, at once, the second, maroon, and he could not lie there, he got out of bed and began to dress and did not bother to see if the noise had wakened his mother, before he ran from the cottage.

Some of the men were already there and the others came racing down the slopes, pulling on oilskins, it was almost a relief, they had been waiting so long for something to happen. It had come. The arc-lamps were switched on, so that the lifeboat and a stretch of the beach glowed like an island, the air full of flying water, fading away into blackness at the edges.

By the time Duncan got there, they were all up in the lifeboat, men were moving swiftly about below, and inside the shed, he saw Davey Ward lean over the side, shouting something hoarsely. He was mesmerised by the speed of it all, and by the way they knew what to do, did not have to stop and think and put one foot carefully in front of the other.

It seemed that everyone in Heype had come out, they stood huddled in overcoats and oilskins, behind the lifeboat. Duncan rushed forward to see, careless of who they were. He jumped off the wall on to the shingle and was knocked sideways by the force of the wind, into one of the wooden huts. As he looked up again, the lifeboat shot forward down the slipway and hit the sea, sending great sheets of water up on either side, which extended, creaming over and over along the top. The boat dropped down steeply and then climbed again, dropped and climbed, disappearing almost at once into the darkness.

It was bitterly cold. There were people along the wall, and across the street near the Ship, and in the shelter of the memorial. Duncan stood by himself beside the hut, he wanted to wait and see the boat in again. For some reason he was not, now, so afraid of the noise and the storming sea. He could not have gone back into the cottage and lain in bed, in the room next to his mother.

But after a time, he did move, wanting to be nearer to people, began to edge along the wall. As he stepped down from it, opposite the Ship, he saw Ted Flint's mother.

Once, years before, she had come to the cottage on Tide Street, with a freshly baked pie, had offered to push out the wheelchair, to do some washing. Hilda Pike had sent him to the door and made him say no, no, we don't take anything from anyone, we don't need charity, you leave us, all of you, leave us be. She had sat behind him in the shadows of the room, listening, as he stammered out what he could of the phrases she had taught him. Alice Flint had left the pie on the doorstep, wrapped in a white cloth.

'You take that back. You get your coat on and go up there, tell her. You do it now.'

He had wandered miserably about the alleys of Heype, with his hands full of the wrapped pie, unable to do as she had told him and return it, and desperate because he did not know what else he might do. In the end, he had walked miles inland, until he was sure of not being seen from the town and then had dropped it into the river, plate and cloth, everything, and watched it sink like a stone. But the white cloth had detached itself after a moment, and got caught up among the reeds, and he had taken to his heels, run away from it in alarm, certain that it would be discovered, and that Ted Flint's mother would come to punish him. And his own mother had been waiting in the doorway.

'You – where do you think you've been all this time,

what have you been doing? That's an hour, over an hour. You tell me what you've done.'

But he had not.

'Did you take that pie back to her? Did you?'

He had turned his back on her, nodded.

'And tell her what I said?'

'I ... it's gone now. Gone.'

He did not know if she believed him.

Now, he saw Mrs Flint watching him. She had come running down from King Lane after her son, with his sea boots and another jersey, one of the men had thrown them up to him in the lifeboat.

Duncan's head filled up with all the things he should say to her, and with everything he remembered, the stories people had told him about the death of Ted Flint's father and grandfather, in the old lifeboat, the thought of the meat pie dissolving in the river, the way his own mother had spoken. For a moment, he opened his mouth and his tongue locked, he could manage nothing, other people had come near to them, someone was talking about the trawler to which the lifeboat had gone. Snow and spray were driving, mingled together, across the open street.

'Mrs Flint ...' Duncan said, and the words that came out of his mouth were strangely distorted, it was the old way he had used to talk, as a young child. 'Mrs Flint...' She might not be able to understand him. He could have wept.

Alice Flint turned her head, as though she had only

just become aware of him. She had a curiously loose, pulpy face, the features in it tiny, porcine, though she was not fat. There was a dead, shadowy look about her eyes, and then Duncan saw the anger rise up into them, her face was suffused with loathing of him.

'You? What do you want? What do you think you're doing, what use are you here, Duncan Pike? You're not fit to be out. Don't you come slinking round me.'

He realised that she had not spoken to him once, since that day she had come to their door, he had forgotten what her voice sounded like. Now, he backed away from her, terrified, and overcome with guilt and shame, because she hated him, he had not gone out with the lifeboat, he was fit for nothing.

Ted Flint's father had died in front of her, a wave had hit the lifeboat as it came back in, so that it had turned over completely and would not right itself and the suction had pinned the men, helpless, inside. Duncan had heard the story, among all the others of death and drowning, as he grew up in Heype.

Nobody stopped him, going across the street, but when he reached the corner, opposite the Ship, he half-heard a voice calling his name, twice, three times. He did not stop or turn, he did not go back to the cottage, he ran.

As he went inland along the river bank, the roar of the sea gradually faded, but then the wind took over, sweeping across the open marshes, whistling through his head, so that he put up his hands and pressed them inwards to stop the pain in his eardrums. He could see nothing ahead of him, but he scarcely needed to, he knew where he was going. Twice his feet slipped and he almost went down the bank into the water, the path was treacherous with ice and rain-soaked mud. It was not far. It seemed to take him hours. He lost sense of everything except the cold and wind and the remembrance of Mrs Flint's face, pushed into his, deriding him, the sound of what she had said.

Where the river bent round, there was a boat, in the groin of the bank. It had a wooden plank leading across to it. In the summer he came and sat here, the boat belonged to no one, and it was sheltered, like the martello tower. Nobody could see him, no one else came.

Now, he went down on his hands and knees and crawled along the soaking wood. The boat rocked suddenly with his weight and movement, and the blast of the wind. He stopped, unable to see ahead or behind him. The river was high, rushing over the stones and choking the reeds below. Aloud, he said, 'All right, all right,' and the words were torn away as they came out of his mouth, like shreds of rag, into the whistling darkness, before they had a chance to reach his own ears, he only had the sensation of his mouth having moved, the idea of what he had said, to comfort him.

'All right ... Duncan ... Duncan....'

His hands came abruptly against the edge of the

boat and he lifted one and then the next, up and over, and then his legs and body, climbed in. At once, he went up to his knees in water, the bottom of the old boat was full. But the wooden seats were only slimed with mud and snow. He hunched himself up on one of them, legs and arms tight together, and pressed his head down between his knees, shivering with relief. In spite of what it was like, of the total blackness and emptiness of the marshes and of the cold, he felt all right, felt safe. He was away from the crashing sea, and from the stares on the faces of the people, away from Mrs Flint.

The wood of the boat smelled sweet and damp and rotten. There were no oars, it had been here for years, bumping against the bank, disintegrating. In spring and early summer, it was full of nesting birds. He had seen a heron poised on the prow of it, still as stone, waiting for fish. Then, the wood dried out in the sun, it was bleached grey.

All right, he said again, all right, and slipped down further, thinking of nothing. He did not sleep but there were several hours during which he sat in a half-trance, his mind and body were numb, he was uncertain where he was or what had happened to him.

On the beach, people waited, sat about uselessly by the walls of houses. Alice Flint walked home, spoke to no one. In kitchens and bedrooms up the town, lights stayed on. Old Beattie sat in one of the green municipal shelters, beside the memorial, bellied out in places

like a sail, with the newspapers tied about her underneath the raincoat, remembering the faces of Ted
Flint's mother, and Duncan Pike, running away.

Eight miles out, the Heype lifeboat reached the
sinking trawler and began the job of taking men off, in
the gale. They must come in close enough but without
grinding the two boats together. Ted Flint wiped an
arm across his face as they swung back, waited for the
sea, tried again.

In the cottage on Tide Street, Hilda Pike slept.

He came to very slowly. It was still dark, but the gale
had died down a little. The snow was falling steadily
now, his hair and the shoulders and arms of his coat
were covered with it. He unclenched the fingers of
each hand, one by one, moved himself inside the coat
like a tortoise, waking within a shell. At first he was
bewildered. There had been the log fire and his broken
ship model burning in it, and his mother's stick, spinning away across the floor, he knew that he had carried
her upstairs and put her to bed…

Then, recollection came pouring down through his
head like a waterfall, people's faces and voices, the way
the sea had parted and lifted up on either side of the
lifeboat.

He began to scramble up and out of the old boat,
in a panic. But he was stiff and cold, so that he slipped
about, fell twice, soaking himself and pushing a splinter into his hand, from the wooden plank. When he

tried to run along the river path, he fell again on the snow that lay on top of the mud and grass and his face went into a clump of it. He was not hurt, only shaken and covered with a cold mess of yellow soil and snow.

He did not know the time but it was dark until late, these mornings. Perhaps he should have the breakfast ready, now, and his own flask and sandwiches, his mother should be out of bed and dressed, perhaps he should already be at the Big House. Or it might still be the middle of the night.

He made his way unsteadily to the end of the path and crossed the last stretch of marshy grass, to climb up on to the sea wall. Half of his mind was still blocked off, he wondered if he were really outside and why he should be stumbling about in the snow. The nerves pricked and tingled, under the skin of his face. He wanted to go to bed and sleep. But when he looked up again, he saw that it was getting light, the sky above the sea was the colour of pewter, he could make out the shape of the first buildings at the end of Tide Street. He thought, they must have come back, it's all finished, it's the morning now. They must have come back. And he went away from the cottage and down the nearest alley, out on to the beach.

The storm was blowing itself out, but the sea was still rough and laced with white, the tide starting to come in again. The pebbles ground together beneath his feet, under a soft layer of snow, and as the light spread up over Heype, it gleamed white in the roof groins. Duncan tried to make his legs move more quickly, along the beach, but they were aching from the hours he had spent huddled up in the old boat. The bones of his head ached, too, as though the snow had been absorbed right into them, like water into a sponge.

He heard a shout, and then a reply to the shout, and looked up. He was a hundred yards away from the point where they launched the lifeboat. He stopped dead. The first light was eerie, and the sky hung heavy with snow, though very little was falling.

The lifeboat had come in, and was grounded at the water's edge, they had laid down the flat wooden skids over which to haul it back up the steep shingle, now that the tide was low. Near it, a few men stood close together. But the rest of the people were still up on the wall, and in the street behind the fishermen's huts, watching, it seemed to Duncan that none of them had moved at all since he had run away from them, and from the voice of Mrs Flint. Now, he did not go any nearer. She was still there, her coat the colour of a holly berry, in the blue-greyness.

He thought, I have to go home, go home, and he began to shake his head, to try and clear out the frozen feeling, understand what he must do. The knot of men stirred, then moved apart, and then closed together again. Bert Malt came walking down the beach and joined them. A man in oilskins began to climb slowly down from the boat, then stopped half-way, clinging to the ladder like a yellow butterfly on a wall. After a time, he climbed back again.

Duncan did not move.

It was a long while before they were ready to lift the two bodies down, on stretchers and covered over with sheets, and carry them slowly up the beach. The sky was paler, like flaked fish.

'What was all that about? Running away?'

He started. She always did this, Old Beattie, appeared suddenly beside him, as though she needed to be mysterious.

'What's Alice Flint done to you?'

He stammered, the words meaningless.

Beattie shook her head. 'She meant nothing. It's only what she says. She won't remember that this morning.'

He looked over towards the open square, and saw the holly-berry coat somewhere, and then it was blocked in by all the others again, by grey and navy-blue, moving off towards the town.

'They lost three,' Beattie Thorpe said. 'That was him they brought, Ted Flint. And one from off the trawler. But they lost another, over the side.'

The snow began to swirl thickly again, through the air, he could not see far ahead across the shingle.

'Get home, Duncan Pike, look at you, you're half frozen. Get on home'

But he waited without moving, until they had brought the lifeboat itself up, hauling it on the capstan inch by inch over the skids, through driving snow. He thought of the things he could have done, if he had been one of the men, knowing his place, and what to say and do.

After a time, everyone went away. He watched Old Beattie, pushing through the snowstorm. He had never seen her without the pram before.

When he reached the cottage his mother was still asleep, there had been no sound through the house to disturb her. Always, he woke first, and took her cup of tea, the noise of his footsteps or the opening of the door were what woke her.

He did everything just as usual, and then left for work, and he did not speak to her once, not even in answer to the stream of angry remarks and questions, the talk about last night, and the way he had gone mad with himself and burned the model ship, the arrival of Ted Flint. He wondered if she would lift her stick to him, in the end, to try and beat him into speaking to her. She said, 'I know you, I know what you're like. Nobody else knows you, you don't know yourself, but I do.'

He did not answer, though he could think very clearly now, the numbness had all gone, and one part of his mind fed orders to him, said, fill the kettle, strike the match, watch the toast, lift, open, close, come, go, so that it was easy, he obeyed, just as he obeyed Cragg. Ted Flint was dead, they had brought his body up from the lifeboat on a stretcher, covered in a white sheet, and there was nothing more to think about it.

'Get down that cellar,' Cragg said, 'get your boots on, it's flooded with water in one corner. And the shed roof's half off, as well.'

He did not ask about Duncan's lateness. Duncan did as he was told, worked the whole day on the storm damage to the house, his head empty of all thought. He did not speak to Cragg, either.

That day they had to eat their lunch in the garage, and once, Cragg lifted his eyes from the newspaper, to give Duncan a queer look. After a moment, he said, 'I saw you. Down on the beach. I saw you.' But there was no expression in his voice.

Duncan went on eating through his cheese sandwich.

It snowed all that afternoon, while Cragg was up on the roof of the toolshed, hammering the broken wood back into place. Duncan stood about below, handing up tools. They had cleared the water out of the cellar, there was, Cragg said, nothing else for him to do. His fingers were swollen and blue with cold, poking out of the ends of the half mittens.

Inside the Big House, everything was silent, the covers straight and smooth upon beds, cushions plump and undisturbed. Major and Mrs Reddingham-Lee had gone abroad, on a ship from Southampton.

Last summer, Cragg had been off for two days, sick.

In the top greenhouse, Duncan had hosed down tomatoes, smelling the dry, sweet smell of the fruit and the dark-green leaves, hot under the glass. The fine spray went pattering softly down through them, glinting as it dried on the shiny skins. He had felt happy, though anxious at being alone, not to have Cragg giving him orders. And then, Mrs Reddingham-Lee had gone out, he had watched her leave the house by the side door, and climb into her eggshell-blue car. She had worn a hat and driven up the hill, away from the town.

Duncan had laid down the hosepipe and gone out of the conservatory. The sun beat down on to the pale paving of the steps, and reflected up again into his face, burning it. Behind him, in a thin line down between the houses, the sea, polished bright as enamel.

There was nobody else in the house. When he closed the door of the kitchen and stood in the wide hall, everything seemed to settle around him, it was entirely still. The sun came through a round pane of glass in the front door. He began to go about the place, very quietly, into every room, feeling the different feel under his shoes, smelling the strange smells. There was pale waxed wood and the thick knotted pile of rugs, the colours of the drawing-room were gold and white and lemon in the sun. He had touched things gently, feeling the texture of silk cushions, roughened against his skin, lifting up a paper knife from the desk beside the window and balancing it. Upstairs, the bedroom overlooked the empty garden. It had wide windows and corn-coloured curtains, and smelled of Mrs Reddingham-Lee, as though her scented powder hung about on the air. He was inquisitive about everything here, wanting to touch each chair and picture and ornament, to open cupboards and drawers and stare inside. But he had moved about cautiously, his nerves alert just below the skin, hearing the seething of the dust. He thought, this is what they have, this and this and this, here is where they eat and laugh and sit and sleep, this is all of theirs. He had never seen what it was like before. The rooms were all long and high and bright with the afternoon sun, but he felt as though, if he breathed out too quickly, the things about him might splinter and break. He touched his fingers slowly down on to the white piano keys and they were cool, the notes sounded faintly, vibrating far away down the strings. He wanted to stay here. Outside, he saw the shimmer of heat over the garden.

After a long time, he had gone and the rooms had settled back into themselves again, when he looked behind him anxiously, he could see no trace of his own presence there.

When he was fumbling to tie back some raspberry canes, Mrs Reddingham-Lee returned. Watching her put her legs out of the blue car, and stand up, he thought I know everything about you, I know secrets. Though later he had realised that it was nothing, that he knew only curtains and tables and vases and chairs, the smell of a bedroom. Nothing.

Now, the wind came whipping suddenly up the lawn, blowing the snow about in tiny, stinging particles. Cragg began to make his way cautiously down from the roof of the shed his legs first, waving over the edge. Duncan put up an arm to steady him. Cragg grunted.

Higher up the coast, the body of the other man from the trawler was washed ashore.

'You can get off home early,' Cragg said. 'There's no more to do in this, and you're fit for nothing. Up half the night. I saw you.'

But Duncan took a long time putting the tools away, collecting up his flask and empty sandwich box, so that it was almost dark by the time he reached the bottom of the hill and turned left into King Lane, he could see the light on in the front room of the Flints' cottage. For the first time since the previous night, he began to be afraid, thinking of what he was going to do.

Esther Ward was there. She had been at the house very early in the morning to lay the body out, and now she had come back, to make cups of tea for callers and poke the fire, and to look time after time at Alice Flint, waiting for nothing.

She twitched the curtain. He stood close up to the door after knocking, shoulders hunched, his hair stuck about with melting flakes of snow.

She said, 'Duncan Pike.'

Alice Flint looked up, eyes small and dull in the puffy face. On the dresser behind her stood the photographs, and the small oak plaques, the bronze medals awarded posthumously. The fire was banked, black with fresh coal, smoking hard.

'Have I to let him in?'

She shrugged.

The last of the daylight slipped down suddenly, beyond the window.

'He ought to be put away,' Alice Flint said. 'You saw him, last night, mooning about. The two of them ought. What sort of a life is that? What sort of a man is he going to be? Cooking and pushing her about and treated like a baby. He *is* a baby, always was. They went to the same school, didn't they, they were in the same class. He told me. Duncan Pike was ten years old before he could write his own name. Ten years old. And I wouldn't trust him, that one, he'd be violent, he'd do anything that came into his head. Wouldn't he? You can't tell me. You've only to look at his face. What use is he to anyone?'

Esther Ward stood by the door, hearing her out, making no comment. He had not knocked again, nor had he gone away, he was still hunched up there waiting, like a dog.

A green-blue flame licked up through the coal, and died again. 'Oh, let him in.' Alice Flint turned her head away. 'Do what you like. It's nothing to me.'

Esther Ward went to open the door.

*

Coming here, down the street, he had wondered what he would say, how he might ask, though he knew it was all right, it was what other people did. He remembered when John Dent had come to school and told them about his dead grandfather, laid out and on display in their front parlour, in the open coffin. 'You could come,' he had said to Duncan, 'everybody comes. They take their hats off and pray a prayer over him, that's all. Anybody can come and look. It's his dead body. But if you want to come you'll have to give me threepence first.'

Duncan had not gone, because he was afraid, remembering the terrible stories they told him, and because he had not liked John Dent's grandfather, with the huge dark warts upon his neck. Besides his mother never let him have money. Standing in the snow he wondered what he should say, how to ask, and began to tremble, the muscles in his stomach and down his legs tightened, and tightened, like pulled wires. Alice Flint. She might do anything, might spit in his face, or hit him, might shout and curse and send him away. But although it was a long time before the door opened, he did not think to leave.

He was startled by Davey Ward's wife..

'It's ... Ted Flint' he said, in the end, stammering, 'I came to see him. I came to see.'

'Yes.'

She paused, looking at him narrowly, and then

turned, saying nothing more, and began to go ahead of him up the dark stairs The door of the bedroom was closed. When she opened it, she did not go in, but stood to one side, letting him pass.

He had not known what he would do, had felt nothing all the way here. The light from the lamp beside the bed, and from overhead was very bright. Through a slit in the curtains he could see the snow gleaming like bone on the flat roof of the outhouse. Esther Ward remained in the doorway, watching him.

When the lifeboat had turned and come in for the third time, a wave had caught them sideways on, tipping the boat and crashing down over the deck. Coxswain Davey Ward, clinging to the wheel and blinded by the streaming water, had seen nothing. Then, the side of the lifeboat had ground up hard against the trawler. When he had wiped his eyes, he saw that Ted Flint had been washed off his feet and half-way over the rail, to have his body caught before it could fall down into the sea, and pinned against the other boat. They had reached and held him, pulled him back on to the lifeboat deck. He had died on the way back to Heype, among the rescued men from the trawler.

Duncan opened his eyes, when he felt his knees come up against the side of the bed. He looked down. He had not expected to see anything except a cold, white thing, sheeted, dead as a fish. But he saw Ted Flint, his hair and the rough surface of his skin were the same, except for the plaster and bandage, and the dark abrasion just below his eye. He thought, this is all him, he is here, and he imagined the brain and heart and lungs packed tightly together within the bone cage, the red blood thick and still. He had imagined something transparent, ghostly as the snow, something that was called a corpse, but there was only the man, Ted Flint, huge and heavy, he could have put out his hand and touched and the skin and hair would have felt the same as his own felt.

He was shocked most of all by this. He did not move or speak, only cried without knowing it, the tears squeezing abruptly out under tight lids, and drying at once on his face. His hands were clenched tightly, until the bones ached, pressing into one another. He was silent.

By the door, Esther Ward waited, uneasy, not leaving him because she had never trusted him, would be surprised at nothing he might do. But in the end, she said, 'You'd best go home.'

He started violently at the sound of her voice in the tiny bedroom. On the dressing table, and the top of the chest, he could see things, Ted Flint's things, and he dared not look.

'Go on. Go home.'

He went without a word, down the stairs and out of the door and along King Lane through the frozen snow, his head rinsed clean and clear, no longer afraid. Though by the time he reached Tide Street, anger had begun to pile up slowly within him, a dead weight.

'He cried,' Esther Ward said, 'that Duncan Pike. He's like a baby. Stood and cried.'

Alice Flint turned around, her voice raised and wild, for the first time that day.

'Him? What's it to him? What does he know about it? He never knew anything. What did he have to cry about?'

And she put up her hands to her face and pressed them there, her eyes dry and burning, knowing suddenly what had happened, and that there was nothing left for her, no hope or future. She thought, I would kill him, he was in this house alive and I would have killed him, him or anyone.

The voice of a man came into the room, reading the news of the day from the flickering television. Alice Flint sat down dully and watched it.

The snow fell all that night and then froze, hard and glittering between the cobbles down all the slopes of Heype, and lying bright and thin as glass, over the surface of the river.

The roof of tile toolshed was mended. Cragg set Duncan on to sawing logs, more and more logs, they were piled up along the inner wall of the garage and labelled ash and holly, birch and pear. He worked steadily all through the days before the funeral, and at night, sat in the front room of the cottage in Tide

Street and said nothing, did nothing, his head full with the picture of Ted Flint's body. Cragg watched him. In the mornings, Old Beattie stood on the beach with her pram and saw him walking up Church Hill. In the wheelchair, Hilda Pike worked at her white crochet furiously, so that the squares and circles were piled up on the table beside her, enough for a bedspread, enough to pack up in a parcel and send away. She made Duncan go, with one of the notes, written in black carpenter's pencil, down to the shop to buy more wool, and for the first time in his life, he found that he was unable to ask for what he wanted, he had forgotten, so that in the end he had fumbled about in his pocket and brought out the note, his face working in shame and anger. The woman, Dora Stevens, peered at him across the counter and bit back her question, alarmed, had read the note and wrapped the crochet wool quickly, wanting him away.

He was not going to work, on the morning of the funeral, no one in Heype would work, people drew their curtains against the dazzling sun and went up to the church, waited.

He had a suit, folded in newspaper and laid across the bottom of her wardrobe, a suit that had belonged to her father. It was navy-blue, pressed and flat, the jacket too wide for him, so that his shoulders sloped down and he looked oddly shrunken inside it.

'That's all right,' Hilda Pike had said, 'that's good stuff, best quality, you've no need for anything new for yourself, the few times you'll have occasion to wear it.'

Which had been, the day he was interviewed at the Big House, by Mrs Reddingham-Lee, and then once a year, when they walked up to the church, on the anniversary of his grandmother's death.

Now, he saw himself, small and strange, looking in the wardrobe mirror, the bones of his wrists and fingers, cheeks and jaw, prominent just below the tight, pale flesh, eyes wide and blank-blue. He had made the breakfast and given it to his mother, put her in the wheelchair, beside the window, and had not spoken, not even to explain why he did not then go out to work. But he could not leave the house without being seen by her, he must come downstairs and cross the room, to reach the front door.

She had wheeled herself around, so that she was there in front of him, blocking the way. Her hair was scraped back more tightly than usual into the metal comb, so that the skin was taut, her eyes pulled upwards slightly at the corners.

'You can get my coat,' she said, 'the dark one, and help me on with it. You're to take me with you.'

Duncan did not move.

'How often do I get the chance to see anything, go anywhere? What company are you, going about the place like a daft thing, never saying a word? You don't know and you don't think and you don't care, you do what you like. I'm sorry I ever bore you.'

'It's a funeral,' he said slowly, 'that's all. It's nothing you'd want to go to.'

'How do you know what I want or don't want? How? You never ask. You know nothing.'

'It's a funeral...'

'I know what it is, you don't have to tell me anything. I read things, don't I? I know better than you what goes on.'

And that was no more than true, for she read the local paper like a vulture, was endlessly curious about the people of Heype with whom she wanted nothing to do. He was the one who went out into the town and talked to them and saw things, and he was the one who did not know.

'I want my coat, don't I? Coat and gloves and hat. You heard me.'

He could do nothing. He did not want her to go, to be seen with her by everyone, the fishermen and Cragg and Alice Flint, to have to watch the coffins and listen to the words of the parson, in her presence.

But she was waiting, her lips parted slightly, leaning forward. He was still afraid of her. The front room felt cold. Duncan went back up the stairs and fetched the clothes, as she had told him, a pain drilling through his head.

It was hard and slow, pushing the wheelchair up the slopes, it stuck in the pavement ruts and on piles of frozen snow, skidded over the ice. The sky was washed a clear, bright blue and the sun shone. Hilda Pike sat under the rug in her chair, holding herself stiff against every jolt, her gloved hands on her lap. When they came up behind other people, she stared through them, said nothing. We keep ourselves to ourselves in this town.

The path was lined with school children in dark coats, waiting. The sunlight came into the broad nave of the church through plain glass windows, fell palely on the stone of the walls and floor, and on the yellow brasses, everything was bare and bright and open, and Duncan was filled with alarm, wanting there to be dark places. He could be seen by everyone, all their eyes followed him, as he moved down the side aisle, pushing his mother.

When the coffins came, on the shoulders of the other men from the boat, the lids were thick with yellow flowers, and as he saw them, he began to be afraid, waited for some terrible noise and for the lids to burst open, pouring blood, for thunder and lightning, and the roof of the church to creak and cave in on the heads of all the people. He wanted to hide his face, to crawl away, lie down on the stone floor beneath the dark wooden pews, so that he would be safe. The noise of the organ rushed loud as water through his head, and he shook it again and again, fearing that it would crack open like the fragile coffins. The sun was dazzling, on the altar rail. He saw his mother's hands, white and thin as his own, resting on top of the dark rug.

'All flesh is not the same flesh. But there is one kind of flesh for men, another flesh of beasts, another of fishes and another of birds. ...'

In his bursting head, he saw the bruise rotting on Ted Flint's face, the flesh, with its blue tattoos, peeling away from the bones, and then the dead white cod Davey Ward had sold him, lying heavy across his hands. He waited as the men lifted up the coffins again and began to move away, for the end of all the world, for his own flesh to split softly open, ripe as fruit.

When they had gone out, and around the path to the graves, he did not move. He had sat all the time, at the end of the pew, his bones locked together and the pain and confusion in his head. When the rest of them had stood and sang, knelt and prayed, he had not moved. Now, he wondered what had happened and why he was here, with the noises outside, muffled by the thick stone walls, and within, the breath left behind on the air, cooling, the dust motes sifting about in a band of sunlight, where the coffins had been.

She was watching him.

'Look at you! You're not safe to be out. What's the matter with you, Duncan Pike?'

He did not stir.

'You can take me back the long way. I've had enough. I've had enough of being in this place.' She waited. 'Get up, then. What's the matter with you?'

Outside, the sound of singing again, the voices of the schoolchildren, and the footsteps back up the path, then the empty cars, moving off. He thought again of the bodies, of how they were like his own body, thought how Ted Flint's skin and hair had looked, and the flesh, dense and opaque, the same as when he had stood in the front room in Tide Street, caring for nothing.

'You!'

He stood up and walked away, out of the church, opened, then closed the wooden door behind him. When she shouted, he took no notice. He heard the wheels of the chair skid round on the floor, but he had left before she could reach him, and then she was stuck, unable to lift herself over the single step.

Outside, ahead of him, he saw the backs of the children, two by two in file together, returning to school, and when he reached the corner of the church, there were the others, everyone bunched together, going down the hill, talking of the funeral. He crossed the road, and skirted the backs of the houses along Cliff Walk, then cut through an alley and down the steep steps that led from the top of the town right down into Market Street. The walls of the cliff rose up on each side, stone-faced, and green with moss. When he was small, he had been afraid to come here. There was no light until the bottom, no sunshine, even on the afternoons of midsummer. Now, the steps were deserted and icy, he held on to the iron rail and ran faster and faster as he neared the bottom. There was no more fear in him, no feeling for anything at all. He thought, I

can do what I like, there is only me and I can do anything. Power surged through him like happiness. I can
do what I like.

In the cottage he changed carefully out of the suit
and replaced it between the sheets of newspaper,
smoothing it all out. He put on his working jeans and
shirt and jumper, and the navy-blue woollen jacket, he
cut his sandwiches and filled the flask with tea, packed
them into the holdall.

'There's that paint come today,' Cragg said, 'for the
garden benches. You can go into the garage and make
a start on them.'

In the church, Hilda Pike was found, and pushed
home by Old Beattie. Twenty years ago, they had
worked side by side, in the sheds at Lowestoft, packing,
had lived at either end of the same street, each had
watched the other and discovered secrets, and they had
never spoken. Now, Beattie Thorpe pushed the wheelchair and was not thanked for it, remembered
Duncan's face in the church, knowing how he was,
knowing everything about Hilda Pike. Saying nothing.

The sun shone all that day and in King Lane, Alice
Flint sorted clothing in the empty back bedroom, to
burn or sell or give away.

Duncan stayed on until after eight o'clock, in the Big
House garage, the smell of new paint burning through
his nostrils and down into his stomach as he bent his

head close to the slatted garden benches. He felt curiously happy, knowing all the things he might do. Outside, the air shone with frost, and a blade-thin moon above the lime-tree.

He did not know what had happened to his mother, and now did not care. Though he knew that he should have gone home. Coming down the hill, he looked closely at all the houses, at the colour of the paint on their doors, the shape of the windows, and it was as if he had never seen them before. There was no one about in the streets. He crossed the square and stood on the defence wall, looking at the sea. It was very still, the surface glistening under the moon. He stepped down on to the shingle. The pebbles shone silver and white, and the dark heaps of fish nets, the roofs of the wooden huts, were covered in rime, like snails' trail. The tide was coming in. Duncan felt again the rich, childish pride in himself, a wild excitement at what he might do. Everything, there would be no end to it.... A wave crisped over. It was cold enough, now, to freeze the sea.

He left the beach.

Tonight, they had drawn the curtains, he could not see who was in there. But he had made up his mind, he would not be afraid now. He thought, I can do anything.

Voices and light and smoke were like a pod bursting open, as he pushed on the door. They had all looked up from their tables, over by the fire, expecting someone else. The door closed with a sucking sound at Duncan's back. They were silent, they might all have been struck dumb. Duncan felt his head begin to sing. He all but turned and ran out, as he had always run, to hide somewhere in the darkness far off, by the tower or in the old boat on the river, he waited for them all to stand up and come over towards him, to be blamed and then beaten, for their huge bodies to block out the light, the fear spurted like water through his belly.

Nothing. Silence.

In the end, someone said, 'What's happened to Bert Malt tonight, then?' into the room, so that the spell was broken and they all came alive again, turning their heads away from Duncan, starting to drink.

He had not known what it would smell or sound like in here, he had been nowhere like it before. He realised that they were not going to touch him.

The woman behind the bar said, 'Old enough are you?' and laughed, her soft pink face opening about her soft pink mouth, though she knew who he was and how old, knew, as they all did, everything about him.

He put his hand down into his pocket, fumbling about for the money he had, a florin and a sixpence.

'I suppose you've come for change. Change or a box of matches!'

He saw that the flesh of her hands was soft, too, and thick all the way down each finger, it was if she had no bones, everything was soft and slack. 'Is it matches? Has your mother written it down for you?' She leaned forward, speaking to him loudly.

Duncan said, 'I want a drink.'

'It's our Duncan!'

He stiffened. John Dent from the builder's yard had come across, and stood in front of him, John Dent with the dark, ferrety face, balancing backwards and forwards on the balls of his feet.

'Taken to drink, have you?'

Duncan shook his head anxiously.

'All right, then, I'll buy you something, young Duncan, I'll pay for your drink.' John Dent was laughing, his eyes and teeth shining like the pebbles under frost.

'Give our Duncan what he wants, then. What do you want?'

Feverishly, Duncan pulled his hand out of his pocket and dropped the two coins on to the counter. 'I've got enough money, I've enough to pay.'

'What if you have? I've told you, I'll pay for you, and watch you drink it. Whatever you want. All right? What's the matter?'

Duncan wanted to cry with frustration, for he would have accepted and drunk, that was how things were and it was easy, and he could not do it, did not know what to say and did not trust John Dent.

'You've got to speak up in here, our Duncan, you'll get nowhere like that, will you?'

'Leave him,' she said. 'He can't help it, he doesn't know what you're on about.'

John Dent was smiling, not minding her.

'Pull him a pint of bitter.'

'What is it you want, now? John's buying you your drink, you put your money away. What is it you'd like?'

In the end, because he could not answer, she did as John Dent said, gave him beer, and he took out money and paid her.

'Put your own back in your pocket, Duncan Pike, buy yourself some sweeties.'

He wandered away, back to his table, losing interest. But looking back to the bar, he saw Duncan's thin throat swallowing down the beer, and felt full of malice, wondered what else he might do. Dafty-Duncan.

He had never drunk beer before, but he scarcely tasted it now, he was so thirsty after painting the garden benches, he drank it like water, without a pause.

'I can pay for it with my money,' he said stubbornly, 'I should pay.'

'It's been paid for.' She spoke sharply to him, not wanting him to stay there, so close to the bar. But he left all of the money on the counter, beside the empty glass and as he went out, he could hear the silence in which they waited to talk about him. John Dent's eyes were steady, green as grass, on his back.

He caught his breath as the outside air hit his face, and he was shaking with reaction from what he had done. Along Tide Street, he wondered why he had

wanted to go there, and everything in his head began
to tumble about, the pictures were there again.

They lost interest shortly, and stopped talking
about Duncan Pike, went back to the lifeboat disaster
and the splendour of that morning's funeral. The bar-
maid took Duncan's money and tipped it into the till.

All that evening, he sat by the fire, staring down
into the pear logs, the skin of his face burning and her
voice bored its way on and on, through the pictures in
his head.

'What do you think I am? Do you think I can't tell?
I wasn't born yesterday, Duncan Pike. I've waited for it,
waited for anything, I wouldn't put anything past you.
And if you start drinking, do you know where it's
going to end? No, you do not, you wouldn't be able to
see. And where are you going to get the money? They'll
not buy it for you, they're not your friends. You don't
have anything to do with them, I've told you. Like that
Ted Flint, coming here, looking like he did – what
right had he got?'

His lips felt thick and numb inside, as though the
blood was thawing out.

'That's what you'll turn out like, that Ted Flint. He's
nothing, just nothing. I've told you about things often
enough, I've told you the way you are. This world was-
n't designed for people like you, Duncan Pike, your
face doesn't fit. And now you come in here smelling of
drink, and what else? You start drinking and you'll lose
that job, such as it is, that's something sure, they'll not

have you up there any dafter than you are now. So
you'll live off me, I shall have to keep you, you'll be idle
and thriftless, and where will all of it end? You listen to
me, boy, I'm telling you the truth, I'm telling you
what's for your own good, nothing more. We're nothing to any of them, do you understand me? We could
be dead and buried and there'd be no processions at
our funeral. We're nothing. I know. I came here, didn't
I, I brought you up – don't you tell me.'

Though he had said nothing to her. When he came
in, he had found her beside the fire, and he did not ask
who had brought her home from the empty church.

In the kitchen he had prepared their supper, doing
what she told him, frying eggs and toasting bread, and
his eyes had filmed over, his face felt swollen, after the
drink of beer. And she had talked and talked, the same
things over again, like a chant, the tone of her voice
never altering, and her fingers flicking in and out of
the white crochet. He was no longer anxious, he felt a
new person, strong, by himself.

The fire burned furiously, piled high with logs, so
that the tiny room was stifling hot, the polished sur-
faces of the furniture were scorched. He sat on the
leather stool, hypnotised by the fire, waiting. He
scarcely heard anything of what his mother said,
though he looked up from time to time, and saw her,
the high, white forehead under the scraped-back hair,
and the white mouth moving, the fingers clasped
around the steel hook.

'You're mad! Look at that fire. Where do we get more wood from when that's all done? You don't go asking for any more. What are you trying to do, burn the house down?'

He hunched himself up more closely, and fed another thin log into the fire, excited by its quick burning. He could smell the soot, carried in clots, sparking, up the chimney.

'You go on like this and they'll put you away, I'll ask them, I will. And then what? You're not fit to be out, the things you do, but what'll happen to me? You don't think of that. You won't listen, won't try, will you?'

But in the end, the crochet square was finished, she cut the wool and told him that she would go to bed. The fire was dying down a little, thick with ash.

'You needn't take all night, getting ready,' Hilda Pike said.

He went into the icy back kitchen and switched on the light. He filled the kettle and waited for it to boil and put the pan of milk on the black stove to warm and got down her blue mug. He took the brown bottle of capsules out of the cupboard and tipped a dozen into his hand, took the cap off the end of each one and poured the powder out, into the bottom of the milk mug. The husks of the capsules were clear turquoise, like cellophane in the palm of his hand. He held one up to his eye and lifted his head up to the light, and the kitchen was reflected blue to him, as though he were under water. The kettle boiled, and then the pan of milk.

She said, 'You watch that fire. You put it down properly before you go to bed.'

Duncan picked her up out of the wheelchair, not speaking. He realised that he must think of everything he had to do, because it was never easy, he might forget anything, the way he was.

After he had settled her and closed the bedroom door, he came downstairs and simply waited, on the leather stool beside the fire. He felt as though he had stepped outside of himself. There was everything to see, a whole world, down inside the flickering fire.

It was half-past two when he stirred. The logs had all been used up, though the last was still burning. He stumbled to his feet, cramped, and went out through the kitchen to fetch an armful more. The gutters were all frozen over, icicles hanging in a clear smooth stream down from the backyard tap.

He rebuilt the fire, raking out all the old flakes of ash and cinder, and making a bed of kindling, crisscrossing the pear logs one on top of the other and then holding the first match steadily, blowing a little, to make a draught. The grate was still hot. When the fire was alight again, he went upstairs.

She was strangely heavy, dead or asleep, he could not tell which. He dressed her again and pushed back her hair into the metal comb, and carried her downstairs. He put on the coat that she had worn for the funeral, the hat and gloves.

Outside, nothing moved, it was as though the world had been bound by ice and frost and only he was free and alive, pushing the wheelchair along the glistening street. Out on the path, beside the sea wall, the cold was like a solid block through which he had to pass. He thought the skin of his face would peel off. The sky was quite clear, arching over the sea and the marshes and pricking with stars. The wheels of the chair slid smoothly along the path, making no sound. Duncan thought of nothing, felt nothing. He had decided what he should do and could not remember a reason.

A little way beyond the martello tower, the wall jutted out as a breakwater, like a finger pointing into the sea. He walked to the very end, and then stopped, and went forward, to look down through the darkness. The stones were very slippery. Below him, the sea moved, the tide was high up at the top of the beach. Here it was very glassy, very deep, the beach shelved down steeply so that even at low tide, this end of the jetty was surrounded by it.

Duncan hesitated, waiting. A wave built up, stirring the surface of the water, rising as it moved up towards the shingle. It lifted and tipped over, and as it came down, he pushed the wheelchair gently forward. It slipped at once, over the edge and out of sight, and the noise was lost in the suck and hiss of the waves. He had not wanted to hear anything.

Duncan put his hands in his pockets and began to walk very quickly away, watching his feet over the black ice. By the martello, he looked up. The sea had started to shine queerly with phospher, like cold fire. To his left, the marshes creaked with frost, the hidden birds completely still. He ran harder, ducking his head.

The fire was burning high again in the grate. He bent down and pressed two more logs on to it.

At first, he was going to pile up as much as he could on the wheelbarrow and take it down to the beach, he could burn it there. He had not thought, until now, that the tide was high, and that in any case he would be seen, the bonfire would be a beacon for miles up the coast, and for the whole town of Heype. So, he must burn everything here in the grate of the dark front room. He went about the house, choosing what he hated most and what would most easily burn, pulling down curtains and stripping the covers off cushions. He took the bag full of completed crochet and fed the squares and circles into the flames. Then he went upstairs to fetch bedding and clothes, and into the kitchen for scissors.

It was the hardest work he had ever done, it took a long time, cutting and tearing and burning and raking out. At first, the sight of the flames excited him, but later, he stumbled a little, through each room, as if he did not know his way about. He would have burned the terrible furniture but he could think of no way, it defeated him now, as it had always defeated him.

He heard sounds first, out in the street, the clatter of milk crates and the roar of lorries, and then, later, the light, easing into the room through the curtainless windows, dulling the fire.

He took nothing with him. The most important thing of all seemed that he should be by himself, the old life piled up behind him anyhow, discarded. When he left the house, he wore only the clothes he always worked in, and his woollen jacket and Wellington boots. From the drawer in the oak dresser, he took four pound notes and some coins, all the money there was. He locked the front door.

The marshes were empty and beautiful. At his back, the sun was silver-white, over the sea. He began to walk along the river bank. The reeds and clumps of grass were frosted over, so that each blade was separated thinly from the rest, and the petalled leaves of clover and meadow-moss were stiff and dust-white like flowers upon an iced cake. Under the banks the still river was marbled, like frozen phlegm.

Where the old boat was, the river curved away through the marshes, inland. Duncan followed it, for nearly six miles, without pausing, his legs moving rhythmically like the pumps of a machine. Under the woollen coat and jumper, his body began to sweat. His head had gone quiet and his mind was blank as the sky, he remembered nothing, the pictures were all gone, the voices silent.

Eventually, the river narrowed and ran under a low

stone bridge. He stopped. Just ahead of him, the roofs of houses, the village of Iyde, flint-grey under the sun. The marshes led away into field, rutted with snow.

Duncan turned round and looked back, and terror broke through him, at the brightness of everything, the openness of the land and the river and the marsh, the endless clear sky, he felt himself standing upright, thin and dark in the midst of it. The sun glittered on the snow, and reflected up through his eyes and ears and nostrils, into his head, where it began to burn, and to make a strange noise, thin and high and clear as metal.

The river went under the bridge and through a field to his left. Then it broadened out again. There was a disused mill, and a low, slate-roofed grain-barn, and when he saw them, he remembered the time he had come here before, he had run away from school and walked. But then it had grown dark and he went inside the barn. A long time afterwards, they had found him.

His legs felt brittle as he moved again, and his arms, too, bent in at his sides. A marsh hare fled across the path in front of him. Nothing else moved except, now and then, the river, as it began to thaw slightly under the sun.

The door of the barn was swinging open on its hinges. Inside it was very cold and dry, but with a faint, musty smell, as though once, something had rotted here, in water. Light came through wooden slats at the windows, in lines like gold wires lying across the floor. At the far end, a short wooden staircase with a handrail led up into the roof, and here, there was a little more light. The wooden floor was bone-dry and still scattered with old grain and bits of husk.

The pile of sacks he remembered was still there, in the corner, nobody had moved anything in the years since he had hidden here, nobody came to this place. He lay down, drawing his knees up to his chest. He felt safe, dark. So this was where he had wanted to be, then. This place. He felt no surprise.

By mid-morning, the smoke and flames from the cottage in Tide Street had begun to pour out of windows and chimney, around the cracks in the front door.

At the Big House, Cragg waited in evil temper until ten-past ten, and then went down in search of him, wanting the garden benches to be finished that day.

A crowd gathered, word had reached the top of the town, and then the men axed their way inside, expecting to find Hilda Pike, trapped in her wheelchair, but finding only the furniture burning ferociously, the old wood dust-dry.

From three miles out, Davey Ward stood up in his boat and saw the rising plume of smoke. The sun was dazzling bright on the skin of the sea. He turned and went on, further out towards the sandbanks to fish.

At Walwick, the body of Hilda Pike came ashore with the tide, and later, higher up the coast, the empty wheelchair.

When they found Duncan, and led him out of the

grain-barn, he pulled the collar of his jacket up, trying to keep the light out of his face. As they drove away, the engine of the car began to make a noise through his head, like singing. They did not take him back to Heype.

The frost held hard for a week, and up at the Big House, Cragg finished the painting of the garden benches, and chopped the last of the logs, and at twelve-fifteen, went into the toolshed to read through the newspaper and eat his lunch alone.

The metal hair comb was found, as it lay caught and glinting between two pebbles on the beach, out beyond the martello. Old Beattie fingered it for a moment, and then dropped it into the old pram and went on, keeping close to the edge of the water.

Later that day, the wind veered west, blowing in soft-bellied rain clouds. The thaw began.